T0063020

It's So Much Better Here!

"Realize deeply that the present moment is all you have. Make the NOW the primary focus of your life."

— **Eckhart Tolle,**
The Power of Now: A Guide to Spiritual Enlightenment

Catherine de Waal

umSinsi Press
PO Box 28129
Malvern 4055
Kwa-Zulu Natal
South Africa

www.dancingpencils.co.za

ISBN: 978-1-4309-0-155-6

This book is original and all views expressed in the book reflect the author's beliefs. The opinions and views expressed are not those of umSinsi Press. We are an independent publishing company whose sacred objective is to provide budding authors with a platform from which their voices can be heard. We believe in publishing information and view-points of different cultures and from different perspectives, in fairness and recognition of our country's wonderful diversity.

This story is entirely fictional and the characters bear no resemblan
to anyone, living or dead

Author's Notes

This novel *It's so Much Better Here,* is Catherine de Waal's seventh novel. There are two sequels to follow soon, *It's Not Just the Coffee* and *Nothing Happens by Chance.* Catherine enjoys writing and her hobby is watercolour painting. She lives on a large wooded property, inhabited by many different types of birds, and finds inspiration in nature.

Dedication

To the memory of my beloved husband

Stuart Angus Morrison

Who believed in me and my writing.

Without you, my books would never have been born.

Thank you Sam.

Acknowledgements

Catherine has used Kalk Bay in Capetown as the background to her books. She would like to thank the residents of this colourful little mecca of artists and musicians and actors for lending her this picturesque fishing village for her story.

Chapter 1

It was the child-lock on the new glass hot-plate that made fifty-five year old Vivienne Matthews decide to move to the Cape. And her son Steven's messages: *It's so much better here. Sell up and move to Kalk Bay.* She had ignored the messages until that morning.

It was the raucous cries of the hadidahs that had awoken her just before dawn. She hadn't been able to go back to sleep, but had lain in her bed in her house in Cowies Hill, thinking of breakfast and getting hungry. Fried French toast, then bacon and eggs with mushrooms and onions … she could smell the delicious aroma of them frying as she lay in bed.

At five am, she could resist the thought of it no longer and decided an early breakfast was in order. She got up, ran her fingers through her short dark bob streaked with grey, and putting on her pale-blue woolly dressing gown, and deep blue slippers, she padded her way to the kitchen. She looked with pride at the new black shiny glass electric hotplate that had been installed late last evening by Mike, an electrician friend of Steven's who had apologized for the delay. Motor vehicle troubles.

She found a frying pan in one of the kitchen cupboards, got out the bacon, eggs, mushrooms from the fridge and chopped up an onion from a vegetable rack, then put the frying pan onto the hot plate with some oil in it. She beat some milk and an egg in a bowl, put in seasoning and soaked a piece of bread in it. She would first fry the French toast, before cooking the rest of the ingredients. She turned to look at the hot plate. It was modern, looking like a plain sheet of black glass. But Mike had showed her that by pressing on the glass in the front, a red light would come on followed by four red numbers. "The first light shows the power is on. Those four numbers relate to the four hotplates," he said. "Just by pressing on the glass you can increase or decrease the heat." He proceeded to show her, and then added, "And here is the child lock. If you press this it shuts off the stove so children playing with it won't get burnt."

Vivienne had been so impressed with what this electric hot plate could do that she hadn't taken particular note of switching the heat on. Now when she pushed on the glass top at the front, no red light came on. She pushed as hard as she could, stressing that she couldn't get any lights to show. At last she realised that Mike had put on the child lock, just to show her, and it must still be on. But how to turn it off she had no idea. And all the pushing she was doing was getting no results at all.

She considered her options. At five am, it was too early to phone anyone for help, so she put everything into the fridge and settled for cereal and cold milk. *Cold comfort.* Now if Steven had been on hand …

Steven, her only son, had relocated to Kalk Bay in Capetown a year ago. She remembered at that moment he had messaged her.

Sell up and move here, Mom. It's so much better here. You'll be close to me and I can help with any little thing. She had not considered the idea seriously at all. She was comfortable and settled in her own home in Cowies Hill, a good suburb of Durban. The idea of selling up and moving had seemed preposterous.

But now, it didn't seem such a bad idea at all. In fact, it seemed like a brilliant idea.

She smiled as she messaged Steven.

"I've decided," she said. "I'll sell up and move to Kalk Bay."

At fifty-five and recently on early retirement as a teacher in a progressive girls' high school she was living very quietly. Too quietly, she sometimes thought, but pushed that thought away.

Recently, she had upgraded her kitchen and had a new modern glass hotplate and eye-level oven installed so she could bake and cook pleasurably. Her house in Cowies Hill had large grounds with a sloping front lawn down to a pleasant stream that ran through a wooded part of the property to eventually reach the sea. There was a measure of wild life. Monkeys to amuse her as they leapt from branch to branch … she had learned to keep the windows shut as they were terrible thieves …. And she had seen at least forty different types of birds in the trees. Kingfishers, louries, long-tailed fly-catchers, tiny little mannikins and the occasional owl. Yes, she loved the peace and naturalness of it all and it had been a great haven after teaching in a busy school with teenage girls who were not all that easy to control.

She had peace and quiet now and a modest pension along with her own home. She was a private person and had got to know the chemist, the garage owner, the local doctor and the supermarket manager. And the security company. These were her backup system and with these fairly personal relationships, she felt complacent and comfortable. Although not of a sociable nature, she had developed a deep friendship with three women, who came to visit her during the week. Not all on one day as she instinctively knew that they would not get along.

She thought of them. There was Jenny, who was the youngest of them. In her mid-thirties, she never stopped talking. But that suited Vivienne as she didn't need to reply, just to listen and to commiserate or smile according to the needs of s the story. As Jenny came to lunch this occupied most of Monday.

Tuesday, she had free to tidy up or shop, and Wednesday, brought Muriel along. Vivienne was interested in the arts – in music, writing and painting – and Muriel was a pianist. She didn't talk much, but did play the piano for Vivienne. Her mastery of complex compositions like *Ravel's Bolero,* where there were five beats with the left hand and three with the right, had Vivienne as an admiring audience. This Muriel, herself not a great talker, appreciated and though not a great deal of conversation took place, the visit entirely satisfied both.

Thursday like Tuesday was free. Friday brought along Henriette for lunch. Vivienne didn't know how she had got to know Henriette and even more, how she had begun to invite her to visit on a weekly basis. Henriette could see nothing right in anything. She was like the princess who found a pea in her mattress ... whatever was discussed, Henriette would find the down side. Of course, when Vivienne told her about a possible move to Kalk Bay, Henriette reminded her of the obstacles. "They speak Afrikaans there, and you are not strong in that language."

"True," said Vivienne. "I am not."

"And it is so windy in Capetown. You don't like the wind."

"True again." Vivienne found the wind blew dust onto the windows so they needed constant cleaning. The wind whipped branches off the trees, left piles of dead leaves all over the patio and the lawn. It slammed doors shut and knocked her vase of carefully arranged flowers over. *No, she didn't like the wind.*

"And the sea is icy-cold, like a knife cutting through you," continued Henriette. "You like swimming. You'll never even get into that water. And you like curries. The curries they make there, taste like stews." Henriette pursed her mouth and glared at Vivienne with her deep-set green eyes.

"No, it's not an idea to even consider, Vivienne," Henriette concluded.

So, of course, Vivienne couldn't confide in Henriette ... not until the house had been sold and the furniture put on sale as well. By this time Steven had messaged her that he had found her a divine small house right in the centre of Kalk Bay, where she would be safe and where every convenience was at hand. "And, of course, I will be there to help you in every way, Mom," he had assured her.

So when the sale of the house was through and the furniture sold as well, Vivienne had had a last meal with each of Jenny, Muriel and Henriette. Each stated their regret at her departure and the loss in their lives of this weekly visit.

Vivienne had conflicting feelings as she had felt safe and comfortable in her home in Cowies Hill and was unsure of where she was going. But Steven had assured her, always, "It is better for you here, Mom, and I'll be able to help you every day. I stay in a lane with my apartment facing your back door, just across a very narrow lane. I'll be right at hand." That made Vivienne feel safe and happy. Yes, this move would be good for her.

With goodbyes said to her friends and service providers, she took a taxi to the airport and easily booked in her two very large suitcases. She had managed to pack just what she valued most in the form of clothing and some books and a few special sets of real silver pieces of cutlery that had been passed down from her parents, now long deceased.

As the plane landed in Cape Town Vivienne looked at her cell phone. A message from Steven apologized for not meeting her at the airport but asked her to please just take a taxi to Kalk Bay and he gave the address. "I will be at the house to meet you, Mom," he said, "but I have some important business that I have to deal with at the office. See you soon."

Vivienne sighed as she pushed her trolley with her two very large suitcases down the long corridor at Cape Town Airport to go through the exit. Steven was forcing her to take responsibility for herself. It would have been so nice and so easy if he had been there to meet her, but he was not. It as easy to find a taxi and to wheel her two cases to the exit where the taxi driver loaded them into his boot. He was a middle-aged man who wore a white shirt and a brown cap.

11

She sat in the passenger seat at the back and watched as the car sped away from the airport towards the city then veered off to wend its way along a coastal road next to the sea, to the village of Kalk Bay, situated on the coast of False Bay.

The road followed the coast line. On the one side was the sea and on the other, intriguing houses climbed up the base of the mountains then stopped where it became uninhabitable, with just green trees above and then topping it all, the rocky summits of mountains. Such a contrast in scenes. She and the taxi driver drove in a companiable silence.

It wasn't long before they had reached Kalk Bay and Vivienne craned her neck for a good look. There were towering mountains buttressed by crags of grey sandstone on one side and the blue peaceful waters of False Bay on the other, with far distant mountains on the other side of False By. *So this was to be her new home!* She noticed the trees all bent to one side and smiled, remembering Henriette's remark. 'It's very windy down there," and she'd heard of the south-easter 'winds.

There was a little railway station and the taxi halted there, then found a way to cross through the traffic and go up a small side cobbled lane to slow down and stop at the back door of a house. It was on an upper level to another apartment below hers. She later found it was a café with a street entrance.

The taxi driver checked the address then Vivienne spied the tall slender frame of her son, Steven, standing just outside the back door of the house. She was overjoyed to see him, with his blond hair, tanned face and smiling green eyes. She got out of the taxi as fast as she could and went towards him, with her arms outstretched and a huge smile.

"I'm so glad you are here, Steven," she said. "I was beginning to get butterflies in my stomach as I don't know anybody here, except you."

Steven had put his arms around her and was hugging her. "I'm so glad you are here, Mom. You'll see how great it is to live in an artist's paradise right next to the sea."

"With you around I know it will be great," Vivienne said.

"You have two entrances," Steven told her. "You have this kitchen access and you have a front door leading down onto the main street which I think is very convenient." *Her new home.*

The taxi driver had opened the boot and carried the two very large suitcases to the base of the stairs.

Vivienne smiled at him. "Thank you for the lovely comfortable ride," she said, as Steven took out his wallet to tip the taxi driver and settle the bill.

"My pleasure, Ma'm," said the taxi driver, and after he had thanked Steven, he drove off.

"Come, let me take you and your luggage into your new home," said Steven. "I was so lucky to find this house, right opposite my garage entrance. You'll love it, I'm sure. It's fully equipped and very up to date." He had climbed the five steps and opened the door. Carrying the suitcases, he went inside then ushered in Vivienne.

The back door led into a very small hallway with the kitchen off it to the left, and the dining room and lounge off it to the right. Beyond the kitchen, the short passage led to the bedroom and en suite bathroom, which was very spacious with a large jacuzzi style bath.

"You'll be able to take long soaking baths, Mom," said Steven. "And your bedroom is equally spacious with lots of cupboard space. And I've filled them with feather duvets and eiderdowns so you won't get cold."

Vivienne took a quick appreciative look at the bedroom and bathroom, "But now I'd like to see the kitchen, darling," she said.

"Oh yes," said Steven, with a grin. "The kitchen. I'm sure you'll love it. The windows directly face my garage and it is small, but well-equipped."

Vivienne went into a cheerful yellow curtained kitchen with two windows that opened out towards Steven's apartment.

"I can almost touch you from my place," said Steven, "as that lane is very narrow."

Vivienne was pleased to see that it had a modern glass hotplate which she now knew how to operate and an eye-level oven. There were cupboards all around, with a neat arrangement of glassware, plates and cutlery, pots and pans. And a good-sized refrigerator, as well as a coffee making machine.

"Everything you need Mom, and I have shopped for you. Most of what you need you'll find is here, but there may be some items I've forgotten." He gave his mother and affectionate hug. "It's so good to see you, Mom," he said.

"You will find it is so much better here than back in Cowies Hill. With that big lonely property, I was always worried about your safety, but here you have very convenience at your fingertips. With a café just below you on the street, and a railway station directly opposite."

Vivienne was feeling tired suddenly. She had been up early and had been worried about everything; though outwardly, she had not shown it, inwardly it had stressed her.

"What do we do about supper tonight, Steven," she said. "It's now just gone 1 pm. I did eat lunch on the plane … and what I'd like to do is to unpack my clothing and take a rest."

"We could go across the road to the restaurant behind the station. The Brass Bell, it is called and it is famous for its fish and chips and the fact that it's surrounded on three sides by the waters of False Bay."

"Sounds delightful, Steven," said Vivienne, now glad she had made the move. Dinner with Steven at a restaurant! After a rest that would be the perfect end to her arrival in this new town. Tomorrow, she could get her bearings. For today she just wanted to eat, sleep and settle.

They crossed the narrow busy street with the smell of fried fish tantalizing Vivienne's taste buds. The subway under the railway line took them from the town side of Kalk Bay to the expansive view of the water of False Bay with small wavelets dancing against the glass walls of the restaurant. It was fascinating the way the walls jutted out into the water with a huge tidal pool in front of it.

The restaurant was already crowded, Vivienne noticed, with patrons with plates of food piled high with, for the most part, chips and fish of some kind ... calamari or line fish fried to a perfect pale brown. The atmosphere was happy and uplifting and Vivienne suddenly thought, "I would never be doing this at home in Cowies Hill." Then an unguarded thought followed. *This could hopefully become a weekly habit with Steven.*

She smiled at Steven. He looked up and caught his mother's eye. He smiled at her with a genuine happy smile. Vivienne again had the feeling of it all being so right. It flooded her. She would have no regrets about moving here. And the first day was coming to a most satisfying close. After that, she gave her attention in part to the food and in part to the waves outside, which were fascinating with white seagulls floating on them, catching the small waves that broke around the restaurant.

This was all so different from quiet Cowies Hill. She knew she would learn new ways and do her best to adjust.

Yes, the food was beautifully cooked and the wine chilled perfectly. Steven looked tired, she noticed, as they completed their meal and made their way back to the subway. There was an African musician playing a piano accordion and Steven stopped to drop some money into the cap that was lying on the ground. The man gave him an appreciative nod of his head.

They crossed the road and went up the small cobbled lane that led to Vivienne's back door. Steven stooped to kiss her on the cheek. "Thank you for moving here, Mom," he said. "I'll watch you up the stairs and into the house then I'll see you in the morning," he gave her a quick smile, "for that early morning cup of coffee."

Vivienne felt deeply happy as she opened her kitchen door. She turned to wave at Steven. She knew that sleep would be easy that night. She was so glad she had made the move. With Steven living just opposite her, her life was perfect

Chapter 2

Just after sunrise the following morning, Vivienne was up and in the kitchen. She found a coffee pot and a packet of fresh ground coffee beans with a strong smell of coffee. Delicious. There was nothing like that first cup of coffee, steaming hot, early in the morning as the birds were waking up. It was late summer and even so, the sun did rise early.

Vivienne had the coffee pot boiling and the aromatic fragrance of coffee wafted out through her kitchen windows and she hoped that Steven would catch the smell and come over. Her wishes were granted and shortly afterwards, a tousle-headed Steven in running shorts padded up her kitchen steps and knocked on the door.

"Hi Mom," he called. "How's the coffee?"

"Ready when you are," she replied, with a cheerful lift to her voice. How refreshing it was to be having early-morning coffee with her businessman son, in a seaside town she'd never dreamed of ever visiting.

Whilst they were enjoying the coffee, Vivienne asked Steven, "Can I make dinner for you tonight?"

Steven hesitated. "No Mom don't do that," he said. "I don't know how the day will play out and I might stay late at work." Then he added, "We have a new colleague, who flew in from France yesterday and I might need to get her settled."

Vivienne's sense of foreboding came instantly to the forefront.

"So it's a woman, Steven?" she asked, with an impish smile.

"Yes, Mom, and she has never been to this country. The big boss entertained her last night, but she will be my responsibility from now on, so I may need to stay late to introduce her to the work and take her to dinner," Steven said.

Vivienne was silent.

Steven looked at her. "I'm sorry about this complication, Mom, but it has happened suddenly. Her name is Mariette." He smiled as he said it.

"Have you met her?" asked Vivienne in a light, quizzical tone.

"Just briefly. That is why I couldn't meet you yesterday morning at the airport, but I excused myself quickly so I could come and get you settled. But I will need to be at the office to introduce her to our colleagues and show her the work."

"And that includes taking her to dinner?" asked Vivienne, surprised at her daring.

"Yes, Mom. It is the polite thing to do. She is French and this country is very different from Paris. I will need to see she is comfortable and happy. But I'll see you early tomorrow morning for coffee."

He smiled at Vivienne, who relented.

"All right, I'll do a bit of shopping. There are a few things I need still." She nodded at Steven adding, "Thank you for what you have done. I'm finding it interesting – so different from Cowies' Hill."

Steven looked relieved.

"I was so happy, Mom, to find this lovely little house. I'm glad you like it. Yes, good, you shop and explore the town today. You'll find there are plenty of lovely eating houses and it's quite safe here. Then you walk up five steps to your front door and you are home."

Vivienne couldn't argue with that logic and reminded herself that she had had a wonderful first day here and that she had told herself she would learn new ways and adjust.

Steven sat back in a chair in the kitchen and inhaled the coffee aroma before smiling at Vivienne again and taking his first sip.

"Good coffee, Mom," he said. "It was the first thing I smelled this morning." He looked around at her small kitchen with the cheerful yellow curtains draped on either side. "A cheerful working atmosphere, Mom," he said approvingly.

"Yes," agreed Vivienne.

Steven finished his coffee and put his cup down. "I'll be off now," he said. "Thanks for the coffee."

He patted her head, dropped a quick kiss on her cheek and was gone. Vivienne sat enjoying the feeling of upliftment she had when in Steven's company. He was her rock. Always had good steady advice for her. He had helped her find her Cowies Hill house after the death of her husband. And had helped to set it up. For a brief time, he stayed with her in the spare guest room, but soon moved closer to town to be able to accommodate the business he was in. She hadn't seen him too often, but she had made those three friends so her life had been stable and satisfying. Not brilliant or exciting, but calm and stable. And those three friends had all had gloomy things to say about her move to Kalk Bay.

No thought Vivienne, I'm not going to let their words sit in my head. I'm not going to regret coming here. I'm close to Steven even if he is away at his business during the whole day and possibly has to attend business functions and see friends in the weekend. She hadn't checked with him if he would be available to perhaps take her sight-seeing at the weekend. The coast line of the Cape with the famous drive to the Cape point was something people raved about. She hoped he would take her there. Somewhere in the deep recesses of her mind she had a sudden thought of Mariette. Would Steven need to entertain her on the weekend too?

The sunlight was bouncing off the windows and those of the houses and cars by the time Vivienne had finished breakfast and done a small bit of housework. She found a shopping bag she had brought with her and set off to explore and purchase extra items she might need for baking or cooking.

Vivienne left via the front door, smiling, as she opened the door with its stained-glass paintings of a sunrise and blue ocean. So cheery and a good note to leave the house on. She turned to lock the door and put the key safely in her sling bag. She had her shopping bag draped over her shoulder and let her purse on its long string fall inside. That way she didn't have to worry about watching her handbag with the front-door key and her debit cards and some cash in it. She could wander and stop at will. She went down the five big steps to the pavement below.

She looked up and was met with the glorious sight of a wide expanse of blue sea. The air tasted salty and smelt of fresh fish. Seagulls flew over the old harbour and she could hear their cries.

There was no rush today. Wonderings and expectations had been dealt with and she had all day to explore this small picturesque Bohemian fishing village and do her shopping. She'd read up on the village and knew that it was originally inhabited by ship-wrecked seamen and deserters, and took its name from lime-burners. She also knew that if she went to the harbour at noon, she'd be able to see the small fishing boats selling the catch of the day. So deliciously charming and quaint!

She walked down little cobbled streets, where there were a myriad of little shops and restaurants, both indoor and *al fresco* style on the pavements.

It felt a bit strange not to know where the grocery shops were, plus the fact that she didn't know anybody. No one took any particular notice of her as she walked slowly up the street, gazing as she did into the small shops. Most were open and the variety was incredible. Pet shops displayed brightly coloured fish in tanks and mice and hamsters in cages, and raucous parrots greeted her. There were antique stores, second-hand book shops, and art galleries. Art dealers, with pictures of Matisse's work and that of Rembrant and van Gogh.... Obviously imitations, but very good, nevertheless.

The breakfast she had eaten had been slight and the smells of coffee, hot bread and spices urged her to enter one of the shops which not only had a refreshment bar but also had a picture gallery. Many were painted by artists she had never heard of, but the large framed paintings had her gazing at them. All so different. Landscapes, beach scenes, mountains and lakes, and incredible sea paintings where the rough waves bashing age old blackened rocks were so real she felt as if she was there at that coast.

"Enjoying them?" a deep soft voice asked from behind her.

Vivienne jumped slightly and turned to face the man standing behind her. He was a large bearded middle aged man with hazel eyes and shoulder length light brown hair and wearing a checked shirt under a loose overcoat. She had been so absorbed in her mind, actually dwelling in the paintings so that she hadn't been aware of anyone else. Never a chatty person, she just answered with a curt "Yes".

"My art is here too," the man said cheerfully. "Over there. The pictures of old houses. One is of a fisherman's cottage actually. It really exists."

"Oh," said Vivienne, slightly interested, but not wanting to encourage this man into further conversation.

But he was undeterred. "I'll follow you," he said. "And when you get to the place where my paintings are I'll tell you."

"Thank you," said Vivienne, avoiding his gaze. She moved slowly towards the next painting of a little girl collecting shells on the beach with her mother watching her.

Vivienne was finding his presence annoying, but she didn't show it. The next paintings were of vases of flowers, roses of different shades of pink, red and yellow all with a very soft rose back-ground that enhanced the colours of the flowers. The reds were more vivid, the pinks bright and the yellows pleasant against a soft rose background. She stood for several minutes looking at this painting.

"Unusual for a painter to use a colour of the roses for the background," said the man. "I wouldn't dare." As they turned a corner, he got really excited. "These are my paintings, and three of them have got SOLD stickers on them. How do you like them?"

Vivienne was taken aback. One of the SOLD paintings was a picture of a whitewashed fisherman's cottage with a chimney and dark roof. In the sandy ground in front was a fishing boat with a young fisherman showing his young wife his simple catch for the day. Vivienne could sense the young wife's disappointment. There was a brilliance about the paintings that somehow didn't tie in with the looks of this man. The painting caught the Indian ocean's deep blue as a contrast with the whiteness of the rolling waves as they broke against the shore.

"How do you like it?" he asked again.

"Brilliant," said Vivienne without hesitation. She looked at this bearded man with a slightly dishevelled appearance with new eyes. One shouldn't judge, she chided herself.

She had already walked for several hours, had found a grocery shop and had bought a few items she needed. There was nothing she had to do except to sit at the refreshment bar and enjoy a plate of seafood soup with homemade bread and a cup of coffee.

She knew after looking at the last of the paintings that was what she intended to do. She nodded to the artist and made her way to the refreshment bar. She seated herself and placed her order, looking straight ahead.

It wasn't a surprise to her really when the man seated himself next to her and ordered a toasted sandwich and a cup of coffee. He obviously wanted someone to talk to. And though no one had spoken to Vivienne, she didn't feel like conversing with this man.

But the café assistant changed her mind.

"Mr Murphy," he said. "We have just that one painting of yours left. We sold the other three."

The bearded man smiled at the shop assistant. "I noticed there were SOLD stickers on some of them," he said. "I'm so glad."

The shop assistant was looking now at Vivienne.

"Our local artist's work is very popular," he informed her. "Did you see it?"

"Yes," said Vivienne. "It's very good."

"I'm Ivor," he said. "Ivor Murphy. I just sign my paintings Ivor M."

Vivienne didn't want to get into any deep conversation with the artist, so she gave a polite smile and turned her attention to eating her seafood soup. She savoured each mouthful. It was tasty and full of shellfish and perhaps vegetables. She couldn't make out, just that it was soft, lumpy, and eaten with the warm homemade full wheat bread, buttered thickly, she couldn't imagine having a lunch she would enjoy more. The artist was also busy eating his toasted sandwich and had stopped trying to engage Viviane in conversation. She was glad of this.

Both ate in silence and both finished at much the same time. The artist tipped his hat at her and smiled. She smiled back.

"Goodbye," he said.

"Yes, goodbye," said Vivienne, watching as his large frame made its way through the door.

Although she had finished eating, she still sat at the counter. There was a bottle of preserved figs that looked very edible. She asked the price and dug in her bag for her money to pay for it.

"You new here?" asked the counter attendant. "I know most people as they pop in here for a snack or coffee. And I haven't seen you before."

"Yes," said Vivienne. "I only arrived yesterday."

"You'll like it here," said the counter assistant. "When you get to know people, you'll find them friendly."

That was good news and Vivienne paid for her preserved figs and placed them in her shopping bag along with her other purchases. Now she was feeling tired, but still wanted to get a waft of sea air and sea breeze so crossed the road and made her way to where she could see that boats were moored.

But it looked like rather a long walk so she turned around and headed back towards the station and her house just opposite it.

She hesitated at the subway running under the railway line. She knew the restaurant was on the other side. One didn't have to go inside. There was an outdoor seating area under large colourful umbrellas. She would enjoy sitting there and doing nothing, but listening to the sound of the waves and enjoying the sea breeze.

This turned out to be an excellent idea and she spent a happy fifteen minutes just watching the seagulls as they lay lazily on the ocean and enjoying the small swells and little wavelets that broke around them. The seagulls were so white and the sea a deep shade of blue. Yes, she was alone in a new village, but was enjoying herself.

Just as she was thinking that, there was a tug on her arm. She looked up in alarm to see a scruffy-looking youth doing his best to drag her bag off her shoulder. Vivienne wasn't one to shout for help, but she was one to fight for herself and she swung the bag hard at the youth's face. She caught him on the head and he tumbled backwards, whilst she grabbed her shopping bag tightly. It was the heavy jar of preserved figs that had done the damage and knocked him over. A crowd had gathered, whilst Vivienne clung tightly to her shopping bag, saying nothing but feeling the racing of her heart and her sudden breathlessness.

"Are you alright?" asked a concerned woman who had seen what happened. The youth had made a rapid recovery and was racing off.

"Leave him," Vivienne managed to say. "I… I have my bag safely."

"That's not the point," the woman said. She was a large woman in a brightly coloured dress. "He should be arrested for attacking you." Vivienne shook her head and gave a wan smile. She didn't think she could go through the drama of calling the police or going off to a police station.

"He needs to learn a lesson," the woman reiterated, shaking her head so that her dangling red earrings danced on either side of her scowling face. Vivienne looked at her, and grimaced a 'thank you'. The youth had by now disappeared and the crowd had dispersed. Vivienne sat for a bit longer on the wooden seat under the umbrella, her shopping bag clutched firmly against her. She hated to think of the problems she'd have if she had lost her front door key or worse, her debit and credit cards.

A dog barked and she heard children laughing as they came running through the subway. Those sounds helped her to stop thinking of her fright, but to take notice of where she was. In Kalk Bay, a place new to her that Steven had told her would be so much better. So much safer. She shook her head. Right now, she wasn't sure about that.

The breeze had quickened and Vivienne pulled her jacket closer to her chest, buttoning up the top buttons so that the chill didn't get to her. It was pleasant sitting in the wind, watching the seagulls and the sailing ships out on the bay and the fishing boats as well. There was no rush to get home and she was feeling a bit dizzy with the fright of it all.

No one took any notice of her now that the drama of the attempted theft was over. She sat for perhaps half an hour absorbing the local scene.

A seagull with its piercing cry flew just overhead and landed perfectly on a swell on the water of the bay.

Time to be moving, Vivienne thought. I'm calm now. With a last glance at the peaceful bay scene, she stood up, turned around and made for the subway and the road on the other side. A train was just passing over the subway and the wheels made a loud rumbling noise. So many things crowded together, shops, a station, a subway, a restaurant and a bay with gulls. Time to get back to her home, to sit in an easy chair and just do nothing.

She couldn't do nothing for too long as there was her supper to cook. She knew not to cook for Steven. Coffee tomorrow morning would be the best she could look forward to. So she decided supper could be something simple like an omelette or fruit salad with yoghurt. She was too tired and stressed to complicate her life.

Vivienne slept soundly and woke in the morning when dawn was just breaking. She could see the shape of the mountains beyond the bay, which were covered in a soft misty light. In the predawn the sky was navy with a bright orange ball of fire just rising from behind the mountains. This ball of orange light threw reflections into the water, and she noticed a deep red and then a lighter rosy pink that was bursting through. The dark navy sky had scudding clouds tinged with gold and as the sun lifted itself higher from behind the mountains, the scene changed again. Gone was the mysterious dark blue of the night with the small slivers of red and gold. Vivienne watched. It all happened so quickly. One minute it was night, the next, day was here. She was glad she had witnessed such a magical change as night took off its clothes and let the daytime take over. There were other shades of gold, yellow, deep ochre and a purple Now it was all sunlight and the mysteriousness of the night had gone. The clouds were edged with gold in a predawn sky. It was breathtaking. Now the sky was flooded with light and the bay reflected it. The distant hills were still misty, nothing definite. Certainly worth waking up early for, she thought as she turned and padded towards the kitchen. It was perhaps a bit too early for coffee, but she could take her time making it. And she also had bought some breakfast rusks which would be nice to eat with the coffee.

Soon the coffee maker was steaming away and the strong aromatic fragrance of coffee filled the kitchen. The strong aromatic fragrance must have tantalized Steven's taste buds as well as almost immediately Vivienne heard the door opposite her kitchen open and shut and then she heard the padding footsteps of Steven as he ran the short distance across the cobbled lane to reach her back door.

"Hi, Mom," he called. "I'm ready for that coffee."

Vivienne felt an instant lift to her spirits. Steven did this to her. They had grown up together and had a close relationship; having him over for coffee and a milk rusk was a great start to her day. She smiled at him as he dropped a quick kiss on her cheek. She noticed that he looked light and buoyant as if he was really happy. Was it because *she* was there, she wondered.

"How did your day go yesterday?" he asked.

Quick memories flashed into her mind, the artist she was unsure of and the little thief … these along with the seagulls floating on the water.

"Up and down," she said, not wanting to elaborate.

"And your day?"

She was anxious to know how Mariette had fitted in.

"Oh, my day went very well," Steven answered. "Mariette is a treasure. She is quick and intelligent. But she is only here on trial." Vivienne wasn't sure why she was rather glad of this bit of information. "A week's trial."

Vivienne smiled at him

"But she'll see some of Cape Town in that time?" she said with a query in her voice.

"Yes, I want to take her on a drive to Cape Point tomorrow and I'd like you to come as well. I'm sure you will enjoy the views."

This was great news to Vivienne. "I'll take you with me and we will pick up Mariette on the way. I have a flask and can bring coffee and some munchies in case we find wonderful views and want to stop for a bit."

Vivienne's mind was absorbing all this. She'd need a sun hat, and sun glasses and Steven would take a picnic tea. It sounded great. She smiled. "That will be lovely, Steven," she said.

"And don't expect me for supper tonight again," he said. "The company always have a happy hour on a Friday so I'll eat there and be home later. I'll pick you up at 8 am tomorrow. If that's okay."

Vivienne nodded. Yes, it was a great plan and she was glad she would be spending the day with Steven, even if Mariette was there as well. Steven sat a while longer, enjoying his coffee and the rusks and smiling appreciatively at his mother.

"You'll find Cape Town really special," he said. "Kalk Bay is an artist's paradise and I know you like both arts and crafts, as well as antiques. There are plenty of antique shops here as well. Don't get lost and don't overdo the exploring," he said as he got up to leave.

Vivienne watched him go back to his own apartment. Yes, this was a new life for her and she was sure she would be glad she had made the change.

While she made herself a cereal and toast breakfast, she thought about what she might do that day. Explore some more. Sit beside the bay and relax, just enjoying the wind and the waves and the seagulls and life on the bay.

What would she be doing at home?

It was Friday and the day when Henriette visited. She didn't know why she even enjoyed her company but, in a strange way, she did. Perhaps getting another slant on life, that of a jaundiced negative view pushed her to balance things in her mind. So though she didn't say anything, she tipped the scales the other way and saw benefits where Henriette saw problems. She still couldn't tell her anything of Kalk Bay, because she knew only too well she would look for things that were wrong and point them out. Maybe she'd invite her down to stay for a week and maybe that would change her mind…. Because in an odd way, she liked Henriette. she was tall with an oddly fascinating face. She had deep-set green eyes under bushy eyebrows and light-brown straggly hair.

She generally baked a dish she knew Henriette would like.

Some while later, Vivienne heard the crunch of the garage doors opposite her opening and watched as Steven drove his white car out of the garage. *White is better in hot climates,* he told Vivienne. *Black attracts the heat, so I go for white.*

She washed her few dishes, dried them and put them away. Then she swept the kitchen floor. It didn't really need sweeping, but the look of a very clean kitchen was a welcome sight to come and work in. That would only be tonight as she would have lunch out somewhere in Kalk Bay and enjoy exploring the village some more.

First, she found a sun hat for the next day, as well as a wind-cheater in case of a change of weather. She would wear jeans and a loose T shirt. For today, she was ready to explore. The day followed more of yesterday, with Vivienne going out of the front door with the stained-glass top portion and then going down the five steps and passing the café. Perhaps she would have lunch there, but maybe she would find somewhere else.

Today, she wanted to explore the harbour with its sailing boats and fishing vessels. It was a longish walk and she was glad of her sneakers with padded inner soles to make for easy walking. She crossed the railway line, and after a fairly long walk, she found herself next to the harbour. The smell of raw fish and of the sea and seaweed was strong. She inhaled deeply and smiled. No, she wouldn't be doing this at Cowie's Hill. She would be listening to Henriette.

A small boy with a fishing rod came running past her, eager to cast his line into the sea. His bright-red shirt against the blue of the sea brought a smile to Vivienne's face. Primary colours, she thought I might do a bit of sketching while I'm here.

Vivienne didn't mention to anyone that she liked to explore places with her fine-line permanent pen on a small book of unlined paper which she captioned and dated. This was a different sort of diary, but, in it, she had sketches from her time of teaching with the quaint old church in the school grounds, the lake with the rowing boats on it and the school itself. Not traditional by any standards, it had a tall glassed front entrance and beyond, classrooms arranged in a triangular shape around an outdoors space used for a variety of different things. Talks, play readings, dramatic productions, small musical concerts. With seating arranged on two sides, the third was left free for speakers or musicians or whoever was presenting their talents on that particular day.

Now Vivienne did some quick sketches of the harbour and the ships. Today, she felt more relaxed than yesterday. Today she was not weaving her way through crowds on the street, or gazing into the huge number of small and very different shops because today seemed to demand that she relax. And consider her new life. She realized she was very alone, and sat for fifteen minutes just doing nothing. Working on calming her mind. There was not much she could do about the choice she had made, and now here she was on an idle morning. But I can't do this forever. She wanted to be in Kalk Bay to be close to her son, who was so busy. But tomorrow she would be with him for the whole day.

In the end She bought a packet of fish and chips from a travelling vendor and sat, eating the delicious fare as she gazed at the blue waters of the bay.

In the afternoon, she wandered back along the other side of the street, going into some of the little shops. Some were strongly aromatic with the fragrance of lavender and eucalyptus and other oils. Others had the strong smell of wood carving as she watched an elderly man deftly carving the figure of a fisherman holding a basket in his hands. So many people had so many different talents. The candle makers and the various food shops.

It was late afternoon when she found her way back to her house opposite the station.

She climbed the five large steps, unlocked the door and stepped into the quiet peace of her new home.

She knew not to expect Steven to dinner so made herself a fish and salad dish, had a long bath with scented oils and went to bed early. Tomorrow would be the best.

Again, Vivienne awoke before dawn and again, she padded through to the lounge to watch dawn break and a new day begin. This was such a special moment. She didn't even stop to make coffee as she knew how quickly the scene changed. After enjoying the dawn, she had breakfast, tidied up and got dressed. She was ready for Steven when he called for her at exactly 8 am.

"Good, you're ready, Mom," he said, with a brilliant smile. Vivienne thought she had never seen him so happy. "Let's go." He ushered her down the steps and settled her in the car seat next to him. There was the smell of leather.

Steven asked, "You comfortable, Mom?"

"Yes, thank you," said Vivienne.

And soon they were driving down the narrow cobbled lane to join the busy traffic on its way to Cape Town.

Steven didn't speak as he drove and neither did Vivienne. She was engaged with looking at the old houses that grouped together and started the climb up the mountain but finally stopped, leaving green trees and rocks in their pristine natural state. Such contrasts here, thought Vivienne. False Bay and the seaside town of

Muizenberg on her right, and mountains on her left. The car wove through tree-lined roads with neat houses behind them.

Soon Steven took a side road. "This leads to our offices," he said, "which are not in Capetown itself. But I'm not going there this morning. Mariette's accommodation is in the same street and we'll be picking her up shortly." Then he surprised Vivienne by asking, "Mom would you very much mind sitting in the passenger seat at the back? Mariette is only here for a short while and it would be good for her to have an excellent view of the Cape mountain road and wonderful sea vistas. You don't mind, do you?"

Vivienne did mind, but she wasn't going to say so. Mariette would only be here for a week then she would have Steven to herself. She smiled and obligingly got out of the front seat into the back seat when Steven stopped the car outside a double-storey apartment.

"I won't be long," he said, and disappeared inside the building.

He came out almost immediately with Mariette. Even from a distance, Vivienne could see the elegance of this young woman, dressed in jeans with a loose sarong as an upper covering. She had long dark hair and wore large dark sunglasses, but Vivienne saw her perfect young skin with slight dimples and a pretty mouth. In a slight way it unsettled her. It shouldn't. This was just Steven's new secretary and he was showing her around.

Mariette was truly charming. She greeted Vivienne warmly, smiling as she said with a strong French accent, *"Bonjour, Madame* …. This country is so different to the place that I live in. I'm looking forward to today."

Vivienne smiled. So was she. With Mariette came a fragrance that was subtle and aromatic rather than fragrant. Interesting, thought Vivienne. I wonder what it is.

Soon Mariette was in the front seat, and arranging her long dark hair on either side of her face.

32

"Right, we are off," said Steven. "I will take the route that goes over the mountains then leads down towards the sea before climbing up the mountainside. It is about an hour or longer to get to Cape Point. That is where the two oceans meet, the Indian and Atlantic Oceans, and you can actually see the line. It's quite historic."

There was a car park at the top of the drive and Steven parked, helped both Vivienne and Mariette out and then walked, Vivienne noticed, with a slight feeling of disappointment, with Mariette pointing out to her where the two oceans met. It was a beautiful day with the sky seeming ever so far away, very high in the sky, and the seas so far below with the white ripples of one ocean meeting the other. Vivienne took a deep breath. There was a wind up here. It was high and despite being late summer, and supposedly the hot season, it was a bit chilly. Vivienne was glad of her windcheater and zipped it up. She ventured by herself towards the railing that allowed visitors to safely gaze far below to the meeting of the oceans and very far in the distance, to the misty outline of a far-away horizon. Somewhere far beyond the horizon was an island and the Antarctic.

If one let one's imagination go one could imagine large transporter ships with huge supplies of food and whatever the scientists would need for the time they were holed up in Antarctica. She watched as Steven steered Mariette around the area, looking at the sea on both sides of the Cape Point. There were big curious baboons and large signs warning people not to feed them.

"They can be dangerous," Vivienne heard a guard telling a tourist.

On cue, a large male baboon came bounding towards them, his narrow-set beady eyes on the packet of chips that Mariette was holding.

Mariette immediately tensed and gave a little shriek. Vivienne also tensed. She knew how aggressive these creatures were.

"Give it to him," said Steven in an undertone. "He'll take it anyway and he could hurt you in the process."

So Mariette let the packet drop and the huge hairy creature soon had it in his hands. He sat on his rump and tore it open with long fur-covered fingers to get at the chips.

There was a refreshment café a short walk away.

"Let's go and have some lunch," suggested Steven. "We can explore some more and take more pictures afterwards."

So they entered the spacious airy restaurant and found a table with a grand view of the sea. Vivienne found herself sitting at the window opposite Mariette, who was also at a window. Steven sat next to Vivienne. She was pleased about that. They were chatting easily.

"Such spectacular scenery, *cheri,* " Mariette was saying. "We have nothing like this to compare."

Vivienne stiffened. *Cheri!*

"But you have fine architecture in your buildings and monuments," Steven countered. "The Arc de Triumph, the Eiffel Tower and the beautiful Seine River."

"Oh, *oui,*" said Mariette, with a dimpled smile. She had removed her sunglasses and her eyes were the same intense colour of the sea. "*Mais j'aime ça.* I do love it. Paris is old and has a strong culture that is entirely its own. The way of life is very different. Siestas in the middle of the day, late hours of shops some of which are open all night. I find the atmosphere quite different. Here it is all about sunshine, the beauty of nature, mountains, the sea, birds and wild animals and lovely mountain plants."

"Do you have family?" ventured Vivienne, wanting to know more about this warm and vivacious young woman who Steven seemed so intent on chaperoning around. Was he becoming interested in her as a woman, as something more than his secretary? His mother hoped not, but had the strangest feeling that she was wrong. *Cheri.*

Answering Vivienne's question, Mariette smiled. "Just my mother and father, I am an only child," she said. "Like Steven, here." She gave him a meaningful look.

Mariette and Steven selected similar simple meals and Vivienne chose a salad with rolls.

When they had finished, Steven smiled at Mariette. "There's a short climb up a bit of a hill with even better views if you'd like to come. Do you want to come as well, Mom, or would you prefer to sit here a bit longer?"

Vivienne took that as a request for her to stay in the restaurant and perhaps enjoy a slice of lemon meringue that looked tempting. Soon, Vivienne could see from where she was sitting that Steven and Mariette were deep in conversation and laughing now and again, walking off and up a slight incline to a high point where the scene below was even better. Steven had his camera out and was taking pictures, as was Mariette. Then they laughed and took pictures of each other. Vivienne sighed.

The move from Cowies Hill had jolted her into a different life, which had many advantages, particularly that her son was on hand, but it seemed he was going to be rather occupied in the future.

Steven might have sensed her slight disappointment, because as they returned and she joined them, he said, "We'll all be too tired when we get back to think of a nice dinner out at a restaurant, but I suggest that I pick up Mariette tomorrow late afternoon and we all go to the Brass Bell for dinner. How would you like that Mom, and Mariette? The Brass Bell is a famous restaurant in Kalk Bay where both my mother and I live."

"*Merci beaucoup, cheri.* I would so enjoy that," she said, with a lovely smile. "Tomorrow, I want to spend it quietly in my apartment as I am still getting over jet lag and need to organize my clothes and papers, but, by late afternoon, I would love that."

The trip back was even better. Mariette sat in the passenger seat in front again and was afforded a spectacular view of the cliffside as the car snaked its way down the long curling road with mountains towering above on the one side, and below on the rocky sea side. Vivienne from the backseat had an excellent view of great rolling white waves bashing against ancient black rocks and spraying huge waves of misty white foam into the air.

The sun shone, there were purple wild flowers growing next to yellow daisies ... all planted by nature but creating a charming scene.

The trip home down the winding mountain road was scenic, though Vivienne had her heart in her mouth when a speeding car on the other side of the road nearly collided with them on a sharp bend. Not much further on, as they wound down the mountainside, a large rock on the cliffside on their right rolled down and onto the road. It was like watching a movie, seeing the rock rolling down at speed and onto the road. Luckily, Steven was not driving fast and was able to pull up in time.

"Whew," said Mariette, clutching at Steven's arm as the car jolted to a halt. "I got such a fright!"

Vivienne noticed Steven patting her arm.

"No harm done," he said.

"Except for my racing heart," said Mariette breathing deeply. And looking meaningfully at Steven.

Steven smiled then turned to look back at Vivienne. "You okay, Mom?" he asked.

Vivienne, who likewise had a rapidly beating heart after watching that drama, nodded. "I'm okay. Lucky you were not going fast."

Vivienne from the back seat noticed Mariette falling back into her seat, but moving closer to Steven as if for protection.

What is happening right before my eyes? she wondered. Is something romantic going on with this young lady and my son?

"These bends are sharp and the road's not that wide," Steven said. "Don't worry, I'll drive slowly. But, first, let me move that rock."

There was very little traffic on the road and Steven was able to park the car at the side of the road, get out and push the heavy rock to the side of the road and out of harm's way. They continued the drive home without incident.

Once Vivienne had calmed the beating of her heart, she was again able to look at the beauty of the scenery. From their high-up position, the sea seemed to go on forever, blue and seeming to reach up into a slightly cloudy blue sky. White frills of foam edged the blue sea where it met the rocky cliffside. An occasional bird flew across their path and the sun shone done fiercely. It was getting lower in the sky, but Vivienne knew it was still a long time before it would set.

Vivienne's thoughts flew to Steven and to Mariette, who was still sitting as close as she could get to Steven. Is my son seriously getting involved with this young lady? She knew Steven did make quick decisions that later proved him to be right.

Vivienne was a quiet thoughtful person. Right now, she was thinking of Sunday evening and what she would choose to wear. She rarely wore jeans and was more comfortable in dresses. Formal attire had been a requirement for her post in a progressive school. aiming to train cultured young women to fit into a rapidly changing world. Her retirement had only been from the end of last year, so she hadn't had too much time to get bored with her new long days with nothing to do in them ...

She decided on a formal mid-calf dress in a good plain deep royal-blue fabric with flat formal pumps that could make for easy walking over the cobbled road. Her short dark bobbed hair with its streaks of grey was easy to manage. For this special occasion she did apply subtle makeup of a base that was barely visible. She darkened her eyebrows just slightly and added a touch of lipstick. Looking at the result in the mirror, she was pleased. No frumpish middled-aged woman, but a confident self-assured woman smiled back at her. She wanted to be her best not only for her son's sake but also for his new secretary.

Although Vivienne had only been in her new home a few days she felt as if a lifetime had passed. So much had happened. She was ready when Steven called for her at 3.30. She saw his car drive into his garage on the opposite side of the lane and immediately went to her back door, went out of it and locked it. She was down the steps by the time Steven had reached her. He had with him Mariette, who was holding onto his arm, taking care not to trip on the cobbled lane. Vivienne took in at a glance the elegant young lady, with the sophisticated arrangement of her long dark hair and figure-clinging short white dress. Around her shoulders she wore a red chiffon scarf. Subtle eye makeup emphasized her deep-blue eyes. Her flawless skin showed no sign of makeup but there was pale lip gloss on her soft lips.

Altogether bewitching, thought Vivienne as she caught a whiff of a fragrant perfume. Steven, wearing dark trousers and a white open-neck shirt, which showed off his healthy tan, seemed totally comfortable with the young woman on his arm and put out a welcoming hand to his mother.

"Come, Mom," he said, smiling at his mother. "You take my other arm. I'll be the thorn between two roses,"

She smiled back, pleased to see him in such a relaxed mood.

"I've made an early booking," he said, "but there's no rush."

The three-some set off down the cobbled lane and across the busy road, to the subway then they walked below the railway line to come out on the other side. Vivienne smiled at the sight of the colourful umbrellas at the outside table where she had sat recently. An involuntary thought of the young thief came to mind, but she brushed it away. That was yesterday, today was a new day with new things happening.

Steven led the way to the restaurant, booked in with the host and they were guided by a young waiter to the upper part of the restaurant on the harbour side. It was again crowded, but their table at the very end had glass windows on two sides so they could see both the harbour and the waves lapping against the side of the restaurant.

Vivienne saw a few seagulls resting on the water, bobbing as small waves broke near them. What a lovely place for a restaurant and with her son as well. And Mariette, she thought.

Steven seated her facing the harbour and Mariette opposite her. He sat next to Vivienne so that he was opposite Mariette and could more easily talk to her.

The waiter presented the menus.

"Something to drink, sir?" he asked.

"Yes, please," said Steven. Looking at Mariette and his mother he asked, "What is your choice? Mom? Mariette?" Mariette went for a full-bodied red wine, he followed suit and Vivienne asked for Late Harvest stein wine. It didn't take long for the drinks to appear along with the waiter ready to take their dinner order.

All three chose fried fish and chips. It looked so crisp and inviting. It was served with salads and lemon slices. While the food was being prepared, Mariette commented on how different late-afternoon eating was in this country compared with France.

"We would never eat this early, Cheri," she said, "and we have roadside cafes that are very popular. All along the river banks of the Seine are artists doing either pavement art or exhibiting art. Some sketch people who pose for them."

"I love art," said Steven. "And I'd love to see that for myself."

"I guess you will," said Mariette with a smile. "I know my boss, who is my *pére*, has asked your boss if you could come back with me to France for the weekend, just to meet the people you will be working with. It is a great idea, *n'est ce pas?*"

Steven looked quickly at Vivienne, who didn't said a word. Her heart had sunk to the pit of her stomach. What was she hearing, that Steven was going to France, even for a weekend... would it be for longer? She hoped not. She had, after all, only just arrived. She hadn't had time to really get herself organized. Steven was her lifesaving rope.

"Yes," he replied. "Greg told me just as I was fetching you. It's all rather sudden."

"*Oui*," said Mariette. "But it will be a wonderful experience for you. I'll also introduce you to my father who owns the business and my mother. They live in an apartment not far from work so *pére* can walk to work. The traffic in Paris is horrific."

Vivienne digested all this, which put a damper on her night out. But, she knew, for Steven's sake she must be happy. This would be an amazing experience for him.

The food soon arrived, as plentiful and nicely cooked and presented as the illustrations showed. Soon all of them were busy eating their scrumptious meal.

The rest of the evening went off without incident. The waves outside were never ending, small waves cresting to collapse into foam as they rushed towards the restaurant. Ships and sailing boats were further out and, in the harbour itself, there was a forest of masts and sailing craft moored, with the occasional sailing boat coming in, its sails billowing in the breeze. The smells of fish, the sights outside, and easy chatter inside made for a memorable meal.

And later, after Steven had walked them both back and seen Vivienne up her steps to her new little home, she had waved goodbye to them both as they went to his garage and soon she saw his car draw out.

It was the end of an evening filled with delight and some uneasy pangs … of what she wasn't quite sure.

Chapter 3

In the next few days, Vivienne developed a pattern in her life that she enjoyed. She was up early to see the sun rise and paint a dark navy sky with brilliant yellows and reds as a fiery sun arose lazily out of bed. In a very short time gone was the navy of night with the brilliance of a new day shining in its place.

Vivienne liked to make her way back to her bedroom with its en suite bathroom, to shower and get dressed before making for the kitchen to put on the coffee maker. She knew it was mildly manipulative but she made sure that her kitchen windows were open so that the strong aroma of coffee would waft its way to the opposite apartment … and would bring Steven along.

Vivienne had got to enjoy these early morning coffee chats that she had had with her son for the past week. She did notice that neither she nor Steven brought up the subject of his impending departure for Paris. After all, it would only be for the weekend. She would find something to do on the two days that Steven was away.

Vivienne had noticed that Steven hadn't mentioned another supper and each evening he told her that he was busy at work and not to make supper for him. But these early-morning coffee chats started her day off splendidly.

Towards the end of the week Steven said casually to her as he was enjoying his coffee, "Tomorrow, I'll be off to France, Mom. I'll have coffee with you, but I'll go to the airport from work to take an overnight plane from Cape Town direct to Paris."

"With Mariette?" asked Vivienne.

She was surprised at his tone of voice as he replied, "Yes, obviously, with Mariette." Then he softened and smiled at her. "I'll message you from Paris," he said. "It is just for the weekend. You'll be okay, won't you? You know your way around now, don't you?"

"Yes," said Vivienne. "I'll be just fine, dear."

Hadn't she been okay for all these many years? But a small thought whispered, *Here, you are more alone than you've ever been.*

So it was that the next morning, after coffee with Steven when he kissed her goodbye, she was left alone. Alone, she realized, with no real support system. No idea of where a doctor was or where other of her needs might be met. The taxi, for instance, in case she needed to go someplace. She hoped not.

She filled the Friday in much as she had the previous days. Exploring the town, doing a small bit of food shopping, returning to cook her supper, to clean up and then to sit and do nothing until she was tired enough to sleep.

Saturday morning started in the usual routine, up early to see dawn break then back to the bedroom. But, today, she had a dilemma. Should she get back into bed and have a long lie in, and no coffee, or should she get up and make coffee with no Steven to share it with?

In the end, she sighed, had a shower, got dressed and went into the kitchen to make herself that coffee. Might as well get used to it. This was to be the pattern for the next few days. Today, her coffee needed to be extra special, in some way as a comfort. But she still opened the windows to let the strong aroma of coffee waft into the street below. Even though Steven would be in Paris by now.

Today, she spent extra time making a really excellent cup of coffee. Strong enough for her to savour the taste, yet not so strong as to spoil it. Vivienne sweetened her coffee with one scant teaspoon of sugar, so that it was piping hot with curls of coffee steam tickling her nose as she inhaled its strong smell. Then the first delicious sip, as hot as possible and just slightly sweet. She sipped and was quiet as she enjoyed her coffee. What would she do today? Explore more art and craft shops? Sit and look at the waters of False Bay with the seagulls lazily floating effortlessly on the waves? Wander a little further? Take a train journey somewhere? Visit the art shop with the picture of a fisherman's cottage? Maybe that is what she should do.

Vivienne sat in her kitchen drinking her coffee. What would she be doing if she were still in Cowie's Hill? Today was Saturday. She often invited one of her three friends over for lunch during the week, but not on Saturdays. She liked to do a bit of gardening, mulching the plants around the house, and watering them. In this peaceful space, she enjoyed watching the birds. There was a pair of those noisy hadidahs that lived in a tree overlooking the house and often grazed together on the front lawn, pushing their long red beaks deep into the soil to find tasty morsels to eat. The glint of sunlight on their wings showed purple highlights and she enjoyed them, if not their noisy early-morning greetings.

'Cooking requires an audience,' a good friend had once told her. She enjoyed cooking and cooking for two people rather than just for herself made a difference. She had so hoped to make delicious dinners and have Steven over to enjoy them, and perhaps spend the evening with her. But this wasn't happening. She had the sudden startling realization that she had moved to Kalk Bay, leaving behind her entire support-system to be with Steven, but was now finding that she was really on her own.

At a surface glance, she was fitting in. But who did she actually know here? Who did she have to really *talk* to? No one. She could phone Jenny or Muriel or Henriette, but none of these friends beckoned her, right now. Their negative input about her move would not be helpful.

What occupations did she have? None, really, since she had retired from teaching just a few months previously. There was nothing she really did. Suddenly, she remembered her sketch book that never played a particularly big part in her life.

But today she remembered it. It could fill a void. Yes, it could. As quickly as her spirits had plummeted down, so they arose. That's what she would do today. She would go out sketching in the village of Kalk Bay. She remembered the art shop man telling her that Kalk Bay was the hub of artists and writers.

Before she went out, she cooked herself a substantial breakfast, the kind she had wanted when she found the child lock was on. French toast, fried bacon, mushrooms and eggs. After she had eaten it, she had to clean up. In Cowie's Hill she had domestic help. Thembi had been with her for years. Here she needed to be Vivienne and Thembi as well.

When all was tidy, she took her large shopping bag with her small sketch book and fine-liner pen and her purse all stowed in its depths, went out of her front door, locked it, deposited the key inside her shopping bag, and went down the five steps to pass the café. It was always busy, serving food from breakfast time to dinner time. She passed it and crossed over the small cobbled lane between the rows of small shops. She knew them quite well by now, having explored them daily for the past week. The shops with the oils and essences that smelled so nice, the art shops with huge paintings by Matisse of his big pink lady, replicas of van Gogh's *Starry Night* and his one of yellow sunflowers.

She knew them all now, including the furniture shops and those with beautiful embroidery and fine crocheted cloths. If one wanted to find a special present these shops would provide one. But she wasn't looking for a present for anyone. It was at that point that she realized she was walking aimlessly up a street she already knew and that she was entirely alone. There was no one at all that she knew in Kalk Bay.

Vivienne decided that she had walked far enough, and found a park bench to sit on. It wasn't far from the shop where she had met the artist who had painted a fisherman's cottage, and she remembered him as she sat down to sketch. *What?* Perhaps this road with its interesting trees that lined it, with the small shops and houses behind. Soon she was engrossed in her quick line sketch. She was pleased as she had caught the character of the road.

She had been taught some sketching by an art teacher at a school she once had an association with. He told her to look at the spaces and to draw around then, and also to leave out what didn't interest her. This was a lovely way of sketching, because, for instance, she just needed to draw the shaggy head of a dog that interested her and not to worry about the body legs and tail, and it did look very appealing. So artistic. She had done much the same with the street, leaving out many of the houses, just putting in a few.

She was immersed in her drawing and started when a deep soft voice said, "I see you are an artist too." The blood drained from her face in fright as she looked up, but she relaxed because she recognized the man. It was the artist who had painted the fisherman's cottage.

She recovered herself enough to say, "No I'm not really an artist. I just like creating impressions."

"I call it art," he said. And then, hesitantly, he added, "Do you mind if I sit down next to you?"

Vivienne could hardly object, and when one got over his rough appearance, he was clean. His tousled hair was brushed, she could see that, and his checked shirt with one missing button was clean. Her heart did a sudden leap. She wasn't entirely alone. She did have a cursory friendship with this artist. She might as well have some patience with the man.

She put away her pen.

"No, don't let me stop you," he said.

"But I've finished," said Vivienne.

"Can I see?" asked the man. "I'm Ivor, in case you've forgotten."

"Vivienne," she replied. And they gravely shook hands.

"I'm pleased to meet another artist," Ivor said.

"Me?" asked Vivienne.

"Yes, you," said Ivor. "Do you mind if I see your sketch?"

Vivienne reluctantly took out her sketch book. It was small in size. Postcard size, but even so she had captured the essence of the street.

Ivor looked at it.

"Yes," he said. "An artist." He hesitated then he asked, "Would you not like to come with me to draw the fisherman's cottage? You will find it worthy of your pen and paper."

Vivienne didn't hesitate. Here was something for her to do, to fill in her time. And she could enjoy the chance to ˌsketch a fisherman' s cottage.

"It's a bit of a walk back towards the station and then across the railway line," he said. Looking down at her feet, he added, "but you do have good shoes for walking."

Vivienne nodded in agreement.

"Then let's go."

Ivor stood up and so did Vivienne. He towered over her, a large man, who she decided was not so much dirty but rather unkempt. Much as if he didn't care much for himself. He wore a large loose overcoat that probably did as a raincoat as well and had a shaggy beard and moustache. His hair was almost shoulder-length, but at least he had brushed it. Vivienne was taking this all in at a glance. She saw his hazel eyes looking at her steadily. She didn't flinch under his gaze.

Then she said, "Right, please lead the way."

"It's back down this street then there's a way across the railway line and then we follow a small lane that winds downhill between the houses. My fisherman's cottage is set by itself on a small bit of sandy ground close to the water. The fisherman who built it was sensible in that if his boat was right there, he could easily get into it and go fishing."

Vivienne nodded her head. There wasn't anything she could add to this as all this was new to her. The path twisted between over-hanging trees and closely set houses with small yards. She was glad of her flat shoes and that she had on a pair of jeans that were easy to walk in. Ivor led the way confidently with Vivienne following closely. They turned a corner and unexpectedly there was a view of the waters of False Bay, with small wavelets breaking near the banks. And on the banks not far from the water was the house that Ivor had drawn and painted. She would have recognized it instantly. She, too, had an urge to get out her pen and sketch pad and to do a quick line drawing of the slightly crooked walls and little chimney poking itself out of the roof. The house had lace curtains at the windows, and the paint was fresh.

"Does someone live here?" she asked.

"Oh yes. Today one couldn't leave a house untenanted," said Ivor. "In no time at all there would be vagrants taking possession and even taking parts of it away." He smiled into his beard.

Vivienne was standing at the edge of a small nicely kept green lawn edged with bright coloured flowers. There were large lavender bushes close to the house with a pink rambler rose climbing on a trellis outside the front door. There was a large brass knocker on the door. Vivienne had the strangest wish to go and knock on the door and see if the owner would speak to her.

"Do you know the people that live here?" she asked.

"No," said Ivor. "I have worked by sitting on that log over there, I didn't need to ask people ..."

Vivienne nodded. "Yes, that's true," she said.

"But I've heard the people in the house are strange and that they would not welcome you," said Ivor.

Vivienne still had the feeling she needed to knock on that door. She didn't know why.

"Well, do you want to sketch it?" asked Ivor, a trace of impatience in his voice.

"Yes, I do," said Vivienne.

"I'll wait while you do," said Ivor, pulling a brown pipe out of a big pocket and lighting it. Soon the smell of pipe tobacco and smoke was in the air. Vivienne didn't say anything. Pipe smoke had an intriguing smell and she liked new smells. Ivor puffed away at his pipe, whilst Vivienne sat on a the end of the log and did a quick sketch. Behind was a very high hill that could be called a mountain, covered in trees and bushes, and definitely not suitable for climbing. But while she was drawing there was the distinct feeling that she needed to knock on that door and to greet whoever lived in the house. So when she had finished, she turned to look at Ivor. "Thank you very much for brining me here. I have had a good time drawing this cottage."

She held out her sketch for him to look at.

"Good very good," he said.

"But Ivor, please go on without me. I can see the way back to the main road and I really want to speak to whoever lives in that cottage."

"My dear lady, I would not advise it."

"No, maybe not, but all the same I really want to," said Vivienne.

"Then I'll bid you good day and hope we meet again soon," said Ivor.

Vivienne noticed that he didn't offer to give her any contact details. No cell number or address, but she guessed she probably would see him again.

He hit out his pipe against the tree trunk and placed it back in his pocket, nodded to Vivienne and was soon trudging back up the lane down which they had come.

Vivienne didn't know why she wanted to knock on that door. It wasn't something she would normally do, but the isolation of her life now was asking her to do something, anything to break that pattern. *A quaint fisherman's cottage. Whoever lived here?*

Crossing the small lawn, she was soon at the door. With roses growing around the door the person or people inside couldn't be terrible people. She would love to see the interior of a fisherman's cottage.

She knocked on the door. Nothing happened. She waited a short while then knocked again. Was this a terribly stupid thing to do? She didn't know, but then she heard slow footsteps coming down the passage inside the house.

She was glad she looked very ordinary. There was a spy hole on the door and she saw an eye looking at her. The eye must have assessed her as being safe and the door slowly opened. She found herself looking at a very tall woman probably much her own age. She had dark hair drawn back from her face, and wore a long navy dress. The woman was unsmiling. Vivienne suddenly felt ridiculous. It was also rude to ask to see inside another person's house. And Vivienne wasn't normally a rude person. But here she was.

"Yes," said the woman in a most unfriendly way.

"I've just been sketching your house," she said rapidly.

"Another one of those," said the woman.

She had, thought Vivienne, a very haughty attitude. She would not like it if she asked to take a look at the interior.

Vivienne nodded her head solemnly. Then she said, "Would you like to see?" and without waiting for a reply, she fished in her bag and drew out the sketch book. She turned a few pages and came to her sketch.

To her surprise, the woman's expression softened. She even had a smile on her face as she looked at Vivienne's quick sketch, which had caught the roses on the trellis, the chimney and even the knocker on the door.

"Good at details I see," said the woman. She had relaxed considerably and Vivienne took her chance.

"I know it is very rude, but your house is so charming and different. I've never seen a fisherman's cottage before. I would so love to see the interior, the kitchen, for instance."

Surprisingly, the woman still had a small smile on her face. Vivienne looked at her. She had deep-set dark eyes with a strange light that gleamed from them. A light that dimmed as it had been when Vivienne had entered and brightened as the woman seemed to come alive, to be energized.

She said, "I watched you from my window. I've seen that man before. He sat on that log for days staring at my cottage."

"Not so much staring at it," countered Vivienne. "He's an artist and he was painting it."

"Taking my energy for his painting," said the woman.

Vivienne looked at her questioningly.

"Don't you understand we are all energy. You and me and him and this cottage The energy in this cottage is from hundreds of years ago when fisher folk lived here. My ancestors, in fact."

Vivienne was listening to this strange woman. A large black cat appeared from behind the curtain.

"Here, Captain," said the woman. "This is…" and she looked questioningly at Vivienne.

Taken aback Vivienne said, "I'm Vivienne. And you are?"

"It's long name. What would you like to call me?"

"Lady Lavender, " said Vivienne without hesitation. "I saw that big lavender bush outside your front door."

"Right, I'm Lady Lavender. And this is Captain. He looks after me."

Vivienne looked at the large black cat with startling white whiskers. He stared back at Vivienne with his green cat's eyes. "He seems to be reading me," she said aloud.

Lady Lavender gave a small smile.

"Oh yes, he's doing that alright. Captain can assess just what you are about and if it's not to his liking, he will attack, and I can assure you he's very fearsome. Large teeth and very strong claws."

Vivienne shuddered slightly. She liked animals and wasn't afraid of Captain, but certainly Lady Lavender and Captain were an unusual pair.

"You see I can communicate with Captain. He is my confidante, as it were. He kept his eye on that man sitting on the log staring at my cottage. I didn't know what he was up to so I sent off Captain to investigate. He wasn't alarmed by the man so he left him alone."

Vivienne gave a slight smile. "Lucky for Ivor," she said.

"Is that what his name is?" asked Lady Lavender.

"Yes," said Vivienne. "I only met him in the art shop where he has a picture of this very cottage and it's very good.":"

"As I said, taking the energy of the cottage and putting it on canvas for someone to absorb."

Vivienne was not feeling afraid of this strange woman, so she asked, "Is that a very bad thing?"

"It depends," said Lady Lavender. "If it is a person on the side of the good, then it's okay, but if it's a person with evil intentions, I don't want my energy to go there as it could come back to me with evil intentions."

"Really?" said Vivienne, in surprise. "I didn't imagine a painting could do such a thing."

"You have much to learn, my dear woman," said Lady Lavender. "And what is it that drew you to my cottage?"

"Maybe it's the energy you speak of," said Vivienne, without thinking. "But I could see the big brass knocker from where I was and it seemed to ask me to use it to knock on the door. I really don't understand why I did it, except that I really would like to see the interior of a fisherman's cottage. The kitchen, especially."

"Come, let me show you," said Lady Lavender, leading Vivienne from the front door towards a large archway into a very large cooking area.

"The fisher folk had no electricity so this was the hub of the house, where they had a fire for warmth and for boiling water to cook food in and for taking a bath in. There was no such thing as a bathroom." She laughed. "Though I have had one added ... at the back of the cottage, so it doesn't spoil its appearance."

Vivienne looked at the thick walls, rather unevenly built. Lady Lavender commented, "Builders in those days made their own bricks and built using their eye to get things straight so things aren't exact."

Vivienne noticed that, but that added to its charm, she thought. There was just one large living room in which Lady Lavender had arranged a comfortable couch that allowed her to rest in it and to look out at the scene outside.... The waters of False Bay and the old fallen dead tree on which Ivor sat to paint the cottage. There was no radio or television set. Vivienne saw that Lady Lavender and Captain were watching her.

Almost as if reading her thoughts, Lady Lavender said, "I have no television or radio. I have no need of them. I get my information from the universe ... or from Captain," she added, looking fondly at the big black cat, which seemed to be guarding her.

"It's alright, Captain. She is not here to harm us," said Lady Lavender to the big black cat.

"Well, thank, you," said Vivienne. "I'm afraid I was rude to invite myself in as it were."

"Lady, I have no visitors. I have no need of them. But an occasional surprise visit from someone such as you is very acceptable. And if you would like to visit again at any time, you are welcome."

"Thank you." Vivienne went to the front door and opened it, going outside and admiring the rose that climbed up the trellis.

"Yes, I speak to it and play it music," said Lady Lavender, "which it appreciates and grows beautiful roses with great fragrance."

Vivienne was feeling more and more intrigued, but didn't show it. She just turned and smiled at Lady Lavender and said, "Thank you, I may well visit you again. I am new in this town."

"Oh," said Lady Lavender with a look of surprise on her face. "And as a visitor you are not visiting the galleries, but are down here talking to a fisherman's great-great-granddaughter... surprising."

And with those last words ringing in her ears Vivienne turned and started the climb up the narrow twisting walkway that Ivor had shown her.

She was tired by the time she reached her house. And what was more, she realized hadn't she thought of Steven at all.

Chapter 4

Vivienne found it fun to think over her day as she sat in her lounge. It had started off in such a mundane fashion. She wasn't one for trudging endlessly up city or town streets looking at shops. She barely visited shops, unless she really needed anything. And today had felt so dreary. No Steven, no one to welcome her back. Then she had met Lady Lavender. Someone who didn't have visitors and must have quite a history to talk about … descended from early fisherfolk. Those *strandlopers,* she supposed, had inhabited the Cape before it became westernized. And people found its charm.

She slept well and woke up on the Sunday, early as usual and padded through to watch the sunrise. Today it was a little different. The sun didn't seem to want to get out of bed at all. She knew that feeling. But really the sun had a regular job to do and it must rise sometime.

But, today, there was a heavy bank of clouds covering the sun. It may well be rising, but Vivienne couldn't see it. It wouldn't be totally dark all day, the sun had to rise. But the navy of the sky stayed navy, with a shifting scene of heavy black clouds covering the bottom part of the sky.

Vivienne sat for quite a long time watching the dark sky then, at last, she caught a glimmer of light above the black clouds. The sun had arisen. But it wasn't a bright and sunny day, it was overcast and felt like rain. Rain at the end of February was unheard of. It rained in winter, she knew, and the end of February wasn't winter.

Well, she would have to think of what she would do today. It wasn't a day for wandering up the streets and it wasn't a day for visiting Lady Lavender. Or was it?

She pushed the feeling away and dealt with her immediate needs.

Coffee and breakfast and a bit of housework. All this took a couple of hours then Vivienne checked her cell phone to see if any message had come through from Steven, but it hadn't. She sat in her lounge and did nothing for fifteen minutes. Nothing but look out of the window at the dark sky. She had time to think. Clearly, this was her new home. There was no chance of returning to Cowies Hill. She had sold her house and her household furniture and had come here, because Steven had told her it was 'so much better here.'

Right now, she would have told him he was wrong. She was totally alone with no roots at all. No friends, no backup of people to call on when in need. Of course, she now didn't own a motor car so had no need of a mechanic or a garage. 'You won't need a car,' Steven had said. 'Everything's at your fingertips and there's a railway station right there if you need to go anywhere.'

Vivienne had just a glimpse of Capetown on that lovely scenic trip last Sunday. Kalk Bay was very beautiful with the sea and the boats and the mountain climbing up behind the houses. And the shops showed the variety of artistic people who lived here. But none of this was what Vivienne needed in her life. Strangely, she had put all her happiness in the fact that she would be living close to Steven. She didn't like to admit it, even to herself, but Steven and she were attached in some way. She knew it even though he had moved away from where he had grown up.

Steven had kept in touch so though she had no real knowledge of his job in marketing, he had phoned her on a regular basis and told her uplifting stories that made her smile and always left her feeling good. She was the person that Steven shared his ambitions with, which was, she supposed, why she hadn't said anything negative when he said he was off to Paris with Mariette.

At that moment the phone beeped and it was a message from Steven. No, he had not forgotten her, but there had been some delays and hiccups he had to deal with before he was free to chat.

Yes, he was fine and yes, he had seen the small roadside cafes and street artists and yes, he had been to his business's head office and met the big boss. Yes, Mariette was fine, but the bad news was that he would only be home on Wednesday. He had to spend Monday and Tuesday in the office, seeing how they operated and how his office could work harmoniously with their office.

Vivienne had a dreadful feeling of disappointment. Another four days … No early-morning coffee with Steven and that buoyant start to the day. That was all that got her through the day, she now realised. She felt more alone than she had ever felt. Outside, the sky was still as dark as ever with a faint rumble of thunder. Could there be a storm coming? She didn't imagine the electricity might go off, but if it did, she would need candles and matches. Best to buy some just in case.

That decided her. She would go out to buy candles and matches and she might as well take her little sketch book. And if it didn't start raining, she might just call in on Lady Lavender. She could think of nothing she would like to do better than that. She saw in her imagination those piercing eyes that seemed to light up at certain times and then to go dark again. And, of course, Captain… she was just sitting thinking of Steven. Only coming back on Wednesday. Sunday, today.

Another three days. She didn't like to admit to herself how much she was looking forward to that. But ahead of her, four empty days. She sighed. She looked through the lounge window across the rooftops to the glimpse of sea and the wide expanse of sky. It was still dark, but no storm was threatening. Suddenly making up her mind, she got up, found her shopping bag and a loose overcoat that wasn't thick but would stave off any cold winds or drops of rain. No, it wouldn't rain, she was sure of that and she set off to find her way to the fisherman's cottage.

In the street, she passed the shops; some open, some not, second-hand furniture, jewellery, ice cream parlour, what a mixture… then she crossed the road as she spied the narrow walkway across the railway line that ran down the hill between the houses until it reached the little bit of beach and the sea itself. A brilliant blue sea with white waves breaking on ancient rocks. There was just a narrow strip of land between the sea and the mountains where the fisherman's cottage was. There were a few other houses further on but for the most part, this was an unsettled area.

Again, she had on flat walking shoes, good for these cobbled roads, and a pair of jeans. She was aware of walking, but her mind was set on making out the shape of the cottage at the foot of a mountain, close to the water. Down the last few steps and a sharp turn left and there was the old log lying on the bit of beach and the fisherman's cottage. With its big brass knocker. She smiled. It was almost like an old friend. The only one if she excluded Ivor.

The sky was threatening, but Vivienne's attention was on the short walk to the front door and then knocking with the brass knocker on the black painted door. Almost immediately, the door opened.

Standing inside in a long dress patterned in dark green was Lady Lavender. Her gimlet eyes held a small smile.

"I knew you would come," she said.

Vivienne was taken aback. "You did? How?"

"I just know things," she said. "Like why you need to come here."

"I didn't need to come here," said Vivienne.

"You were drawn here," said Lady Lavender.

"I don't know what you call it, but it seemed the right thing for me to do today."

"And it is," said Lady Lavender, opening the door widely. The big black cat appeared from behind her.

"No trouble, Captain. It's our new friend. Please come in." She graciously stood to one side, whilst Vivienne came inside.

Just then, there came a flash of lightning. "Yes, a storm coming," said Lady Lavender.

For the first time, Vivienne was alarmed. She had been so intent on coming here that the storm didn't strike her as being a bother.

Another flash of lightening and a roll of thunder.

"Come, let's shut the door," said Lady Lavender. "Would you like a cup of tea after that walk? Or what I drink is ginger tea … ginger with honey."

"That sounds interesting," said Vivienne. "Please may I join you with that?"

"Then let's first go to the kitchen and get ourselves a cup of ginger tea and some fisherman's cookies. Special ones I make from an old recipe of my mother's."

Vivienne found a high black stool on which to sit, whilst she watched Lady Lavender cut several slices off a big piece of raw root ginger and place them in each of two cups. Then she added boiling water, and a large spoonful of honey.

"Let it brew for a few minutes, then taste it," she said.

Vivienne was surprised at the smooth way in which Lady Lavender accommodated her, with such command and ease, as if she had a constant stream of visitors.

There were some brilliant flashes of lightning, followed by a huge crash of thunder.

"It will be better when the rain comes," said Lady Lavender. "It's going to be quite a storm. I trust the fishing boats are all safely back in the harbour."

More flashes of lightning, and more big cracks of thunder sounded. Lady Lavender was unconcerned. She picked up her cup of ginger tea and put some cookies on a plate and indicated that Vivienne should do the same.

"Come," she said, just as another brilliant flash of lightning seemed to come right into the cottage.

Vivienne was mildly ruffled. She hadn't really expected it to rain or to storm though the sky had looked threatening from before dawn, but that was because she wasn't thinking past coming to Lavender cottage. She followed Lady Lavender and together they were seated. Now the storm was really raging.

"Try your tea," said Lady Lavender. "Don't worry about the storm. It may go on for hours."

At this Vivienne felt really worried. Walking back in such a storm would be stupid.

"You can always stay with me," said Lady Lavender. "So please stop worrying. We have much to talk about. I have been waiting for you for a long time."

Vivienne was even more surprised at this, but took a sip of the tea. It was delicious and she relaxed.

"Stay with you?" she asked.

"Yes, but the thunder and lightning are stopping. We just have the rain, for how long I am not sure. But the earth is always pleased to receive blessings from heaven."

So Vivienne leant back in her chair. She realised that what was really important was inside the cottage, her sitting with Lady Lavender who had been expecting her for a long time….

How had this happened? It was when she sat on that bench to draw and Ivor turned up. The walk to the fisherman's cottage. The visit to Lady Lavender. She seemed to be able to see those strange, worrisome thoughts that kept popping into Vivienne's head.

Lady Lavender was looking at her and Vivienne felt a slight shiver. And then that enormous black cat. It also had staring eyes that seemed to rivet into a person. All the same, it didn't have a scary feel to Vivienne. She almost felt she had broken some kind of barrier and that this woman would share some secrets with her.

Vivienne was seated on a comfy armchair that had a view through the small window of the pelting rain and of the small path, which was now a raging river.

"Just observe without thinking," said Lady Lavender. "Don't label it anything. Just enjoy being here."

This wasn't easy to do as worrisome thoughts kept popping into Vivienne's head.

"Just watch your thoughts, Vivienne. Close your eyes if you wish. Your thoughts will disappear. I want you and I to have a chat."

The scene outside was frightening. Vivienne could no longer see the sea or the bay for the blanket of rain covering her view. She did as Lady Lavender asked.

Surprisingly, she found her mind was peaceful and she opened her eyes. The worried look on her face had given rise to a relaxed look and even a smile.

"I imagine things could be worse," she said.

"Don't even say that," said Lady Lavender. "Here you and I are sitting with ginger tea and biscuits safe and warm. Be happy. What is happening outside is of no concern to you."

Vivienne sighed and smiled.

"Good, you are here now in this room with me. Not scattered outside," and Lady Lavender gave her a faint smile.

"Do you know the saying, when the pupil is ready the teacher will appear?"

Vivienne hadn't. Hadn't she been a teacher herself until recently?

Lady Lavender honed into her thoughts. "No, Vivienne I'm not talking about *you* as a teacher. That is your ego talking. I'm talking about you as a student. A student of mine for things in yourself. One thing very strong in you is your *ego*. You are going to have to work very hard to get it under control."

Vivienne was nonplussed. This wasn't the kind of chat she had imagined having with Lady Lavender. She imagined her telling her thrilling tales of fishermen lost at sea, of pirate ships and beautiful sailing ships and tales of where her original family had come from. She hadn't imagined there was anything wrong with her at all. Except perhaps it was a stupid move of hers to come here from her comfortable life in Cowies hill.

"Sometimes we can get too settled, too much in a comfort zone. In a rut you could call it." Lady Lavender again seemed to know what she was thinking.

"Oh, I agree. I have been jolted out of it," said Vivienne, now on the defensive. "I was nicely settled in Cowies Hill with a well-organized and smoothly running life, ordered, peaceful life – and now I have this."

"Yes, you are here and it is important that you *be* here. With me in this room and not in Cowies Hill," said Lady Lavender. "Or waiting for your son."

How did she know that? wondered Vivienne. She gave a small smile and said, "You are right. I am here and you are quite right. Nothing else should matter."

"That's exactly it. Nothing else does matter. This is your first lesson. How do you like ginger tea?"

Vivienne sat, enjoying the biscuit. She could taste spices, cinnamon and the faintest taste of cloves in a soft biscuit with a distinct buttery flavour. The taste was all she was aware of.

"Good," said Lady Lavender. "You are learning the lesson correctly. There is only Now. No tomorrow or yesterday. Now is all you have."

Vivienne looked at her in surprise.

"Yes, savour the now."

Vivienne smiled. The biscuit was delicious and the ginger tea with the strong taste of honey was refreshing. She took a sip of tea. All she concentrated on now was the flavour of the tea.

"That's right," encouraged Lady Lavender. "That's all you have."

Into Vivienne's mind flashed the disappointment of Steven's absence.

"Stay in the moment," commanded Lady Lavender. "You are wandering."

Vivienne jumped. She smiled woefully.

"You are here and did you notice? The rain has stopped."

Vivienne hadn't noticed. She'd been drinking ginger tea and eating spicy biscuits in a room with a strange woman.

"I'm not such a stranger, Vivienne," said Lady Lavender, to Vivienne's chagrin. "We have been here together before, but this is a new journey."

Vivienne looked at her in surprise.

"You will be able to go home safely," said Lady Lavender. "The rain has stopped and the river outside has lowered and the path is visible."

Vivienne felt that small talk was inappropriate... asking her about her heritage was quite out of place. She stayed silent, enjoying the last of her tea and biscuit.

"Don't think today was a waste of time, Vivienne. It's very valuable. I have enjoyed having you here." She gave a rare smile.

Vivienne breathed deeply. "It has been kind of you," she said.

"No kindness. Just a lesson for us both. Me in tuning in to you and you in awareness."

Vivienne glanced outside. Though the sky ws still dull, she could see the shimmer of the water of False Bay and the ocean. She saw the outline of the old dead tree she had sat on was it only yesterday, to draw this cottage.

And she looked up and smiled. The heavy black clouds that had been there this morning had gone. A soft blue sky smiled at her. She smiled back with a wonderful feeling of peace and freedom. It was momentary, but it felt good.

And she knew despite that heavy black sky of early morning, she had done the right thing by coming here.

She picked up her cup and plate. "I'll take them to the kitchen then I'll be on my way." She smiled at Lady Lavender and at the big black cat that was regarding her warily. "I have been in the right place at the right time, thank you."

And she made her way to the kitchen then to the front door.

Lady Lavender gave a small wave of her hand and Vivienne responded with a smile as her canvas shoes met the damp earth. My feet will be wet in no time, she thought. She climbed up the steps quickly and went across the railway line and then she was back on the street not far from her home.

Chapter 5

Back home, Vivienne had a hot bath in which she indulged herself by adding some scented oils. She lay in the water, remembering the good lesson Lady Lavender had taught her today.

There is only this moment. Enjoy it. She splashed her hands in the scented water, creating bubbles. Foam really. She lay back in the warm foam and smiled. Strange she could smile now. She needed to remember that lesson. Steven might not be home, but she was in good spirits.

What to eat …? Never mind that she was on her own. Tonight, was a celebration. She had spent an entire day without her mind wandering more than once to her son. And the feeling she was pushing away was that he had told her it was so much better here when she was feeling that it wasn't.

Chicken a la king with cream and a salad seasoned perfectly. She ate it thinking only of the meal. Lesson learnt.

After eating and keeping herself in the moment, Vivienne found a dvd in the collection left by the previous owner and enjoyed her evening. Her sleep was wonderful and Monday saw her up to enjoy another beautiful sunrise.

But it wasn't so easy to stay in the moment when she had no idea what to do with her time. She wouldn't visit Lady Lavender today. She couldn't impose on her. So the day lay ahead with nothing to spend her time on. Vivienne had always tried to fill her life with meaning. But after coffee and breakfast what was she to do? Housework? An hour would have everything beautifully in order.

How was she going to spend her life? Steven's absence was a shock and was throwing her back on her own devices.

No, she wouldn't sketch today. A bit of food shopping could be useful. That would take up some time. Then there was lunch to make and she could have a rest. Not that she was tired.

What a mess her life had become. *Stay in the moment… and give your life meaning … it's all you have.* She thought about that. It was interesting to think that each moment made the present; and the past and the future all came together in the present moment.

But philosophizing wasn't going to give meaning to her life. She felt frustrated and down in the dumps.

No Steven for early morning coffee and, yes, a deadly boring day ahead. Breakfast. Shopping and then home for lunch and for a rest when I am not tired. What should I do?

If I go shopping, I will be trailing around, carrying a heavy package. Steven can do that for me on Wednesday. It's the least he can do, she thought

Then what should I do? Perhaps she should sit with a piece of paper and just explore her possibilities. *But why would I want to do that? For no other reason than that I don't want to waste my energy shopping, because I have nothing to do.*

Here I am in a new village sitting opposite a railway line that maybe goes somewhere interesting. At that moment a train zoomed along the railway line … the view from her window was of a yellow snake-like train.

The station was directly opposite. *Why not take a train journey somewhere?* It didn't matter where. It at least would be something new.

Her mind made up, she felt a lift of the spirits again. Stay in the moment and enjoy life. A train trip would be better than trudging the streets shopping for food.

Across at the station, she found herself in a dilemma. North to Capetown or south to smaller villages on this route. She knew there was Fish Hoek and then Simonstown. The naval base. Didn't they have just one ship? She smiled at the thought and bought a return ticket to Simonstown.

The next train was due shortly. It came in with speed, stopped and the doors opened silently. Vivienne hadn't been in a train in a very long time so this was quite exciting to her. She smiled as she chose a seat on the left side with a view of the coastline and the sea, while mountains loomed up on her right.

The train started moving, gathering speed as it travelled south towards Simonstown. She looked with delight at the blue sea almost right up against the train lines. It was if she could jump from the window of the train and land up on the beach.

Ridiculous, but she was enjoying herself. The rhythmic sound of the wheels on the railway lines lulled her busy mind. Stay in the moment, she said to herself, looking out of the window to capture as many images as she could. The sky was blue today, no clouds.

Okay, I now have just that thought. Vivienne jerked as the train came to a halt. Fish Hoek, she read on the station sign board. The blue sea was full of fish. She hadn't she seen seals yesterday and she wondered if she would today. They were special.

The train whistled and drew off at speed. Vivienne continued to enjoy the changing scene. Mountains on her right, high and craggy. With forests below and here, on her left, the endless blue sea with curving coastline with frills of white foam as the waves broke against rocks or onto the shore.

Then the train halted. Vivienne looked up. They had reached Simonstown. Her return ticket was for a train back to Kalk Bay in three hours' time. What to do in those three hours? She alighted from the train and looked around.

Outside the station, she halted to read a postcard inviting visitors to visit the penguin colony at Boulders. She looked at the picture of stately penguins in important black and white business suits as they went about their portly business and she smiled. Yes, that would be fun but how far was Boulders? How would she get there?

She was standing in front of the placard considering what to do when a hand touched her shoulder. She turned quickly. An elderly man with quizzical blue eyes was observing her.

"Lady, would you like transport to go and see the penguins? I am Ted and I run a taxi service. I can take you there and bring you back if that is what you would like."

"Yes please," said Vivienne, turning to observe the red car with the sign taxi on its roof.

Vivienne smiled at Ted. Wasn't life so great at this moment? A taxi to the penguins several kilometres further on.

He quoted her a price which she paid him and then she settled herself on the back seat. In fifteen minutes, Ted dropped her off, commenting that he would pick her up from this spot in two hours' time. Ted left Vivienne just outside the café above Boulders Beach. This she wasn't interested in at the moment. Later, after watching the penguins it would be good to get a cup of coffee here. For now, she all clustered together off to discover the joys of Boulders' penguins.

Walking along a path, down some steps, around a corner and going through a pay-gate, Vivienne reached the rocky terrain of the penguins. She could see where the name came from as she looked at great boulders clustered together. She smiled as she watched the self-contained penguins. *I am aware and I am in this moment,* she said to herself as dignified penguins waddled over the rocks to the water. Vivienne looked at the sea swirling around huge rocks, savouring the smells, the cries of the seagulls, the soft swish of the ocean as it washed against the rocks and found its way in between them. Some penguins were enjoying a splash in the water. Others seemed to be having a meeting as a small group clustered together like important business men in their black suits. Vivienne smiled. She had always loved pictures of penguins and here she was amongst them. They walked so awkwardly, she noticed, but that didn't take away from their dignity. How blessed was this coast to have such rare birds that had confidence in visitors and didn't fly off. Yes, at this moment it was much better here! She took hold of her wandering mind No nothing else mattered. Just her being here in the middle of a penguin colony.

She spent a long time watching the comings and goings of the penguins. She sat in the warm sun on a rock doing nothing. She did have a momentary thought of Steven, but immediately brought her thoughts back to this moment and to a silence in her head where she was observing, without thinking, the ancient old tall rocks with barnacles encrusted on them. The foaming ever-moving sea and the dozens of penguins all engaged in their own pursuits.

Vivienne looked up at the screech of a seagull and inhaled the salty air of the sea. *How special!* She watched the little busy birds as they waddled about and climbed the rocks to reach the sandy beach. They looked so awkward until they reached the water. An hour went past easily as Vivienne sat on the rocks, being part of the pantomime in front of her. The blue of the sea, an innocent lighter blue sky, the cream sandy beach and the serene colony of birds.

It was strange to sit so still for so long without the feeling of being bored or needing to get up and do something. After a long time, she sighed deeply. Time to move, she thought, and made her way back to the restaurant for a light lunch and coffee. She was ready for Ted when he arrived on time to take her back to Simonstown train station.

She paid Ted for the return trip and gave him a generous tip, with a smile and thanking him for the extra special day she had had.

Her trip back in the train was likewise peaceful and when she entered her new little home, she felt glad that the day had gone so well. She slept peacefully that night.

Dawn, the next day, was breathtaking. She smiled at the golden sun shining over the expanse of sea and felt a satisfaction in knowing that Steven would be home the next day.

But the feeling of disappointment began as she made her first cup of coffee and drank it alone. She liked to tell herself that after tomorrow morning, things would be back to normal., but today, she felt depressed. She looked into the cup of coffee. There were some small white bubbles at the sides and she swirled them about, for no reason except that the day didn't feel so good. The aroma of coffee tickled her nostrils, but today it didn't excite her. Was the whole day to feel colourless, like it did now? Slowly, she took a sip. The coffee did taste good, but not good enough to cheer her up. Stay in the moment, it's all you have, she remembered Lady Lavender saying to her.

This moment wasn't one she wanted to live in, she thought. Why had she left her ordered life in Cowies Hill, where she knew what interesting things she would do each day. She took a sip of the hot coffee. What was she to do today? Definitely not visit Lady Lavender. She felt a bit like a school girl who had new lessons to learn and she didn't really like them. Lady Lavender wasn't someone to get friendly with. She would be polite and make Vivienne feel comfortable, but the conversation didn't go the way Vivienne had wanted it to go.

Yesterday was lovely, but she couldn't keep taking train journeys here and there. And anyway, she doubted there could be anything as nice as those penguins yesterday. She gave a smile as she thought of the awkward little black-coated gentlemen and gentlewomen waddling off to the sea. And she couldn't keep thinking of yesterday, because yesterday was gone and she was faced with today.

She solemnly drank her coffee, keeping her mind off worrisome things. Keep it silent, she thought. Nothing in it. Just concentrate on finishing the coffee and getting showered and ready for the day. She would decide what to do after she had had breakfast.

An hour later, having to a degree kept her mind onto the chore at hand, be it making or eating breakfast or cleaning up afterwards, she was ready for the day. She gave a huge sigh. She might just go back to bed and sleep for the rest of the day. That was one option, but she dismissed it.

What to do? Sweep, dust, polish, clean in corners, check out her clothes, see nothing needed mending. What a bore? But at least it would keep her busy. She just had to get through today and Steven would be home tomorrow for dinner.

Much better here, she remembered his words. Right now, it wasn't, but at that moment, her cell phone beeped. A message from Steven. Arriving 8.30 tomorrow morning. Lots to tell you Mom. Love, Steven.

Well, that was at least something, she thought, and for the rest of the day, I will stay indoors and clean and tidy and perhaps cook something for dinner tonight, and maybe for tomorrow as well. Or would Steven take her out to dinner perhaps? She perked up at the thought.

Her day indoors was one where she did a thorough job as a housewife, something she'd forgotten as Thembi back in Cowies hill did all this for her. She did have the television to watch, but found it so boring. Politics and people getting arrested and doing wrong things. Really, what was wrong with society?

In the end, she found another dvd that was slightly humourous and she felt cheered at the thought of Steven arriving early the next morning. It was a dreary day, but better, she thought, than idly wandering up the street looking at the shops.

She ate dinner early, cleaned up and watched another film. Was this all there was to life? Stay in the moment, it's all you have. Not very cheering, she thought grumpily, and went to bed. Sleep didn't come easily and when it did come, it brought bad dreams. Steven keeping on waving at her, but not getting any closer. She was glad to wake up early and greet the dawn.

Not so long now before Steven arrived. She hoped he would drop off Mariette before he came home. She wanted him to herself. Definitely.

It was 10.30 before she saw his white car pull up and enter the garage opposite. Her heart sang a song of delight and she was one big smile when her handsome son got out and came over to see her.

"Mom, how have you been?" he asked, kissing her on the cheek.

She hugged him in return. It was so good to feel his solid body in her arms. So reassuring. She didn't like to admit it, but she felt very close to tears; her emotions were in such turmoil.

"Coffee, Steven? I have the filtered coffee ready-made. Just need to heat it."

"Yes, Mom, that would be great and can we perhaps sit in the lounge whilst I fill you in? Might as well be comfortable."

Vivienne heated the coffee and took out some cream biscuits to her son who was seated in the lounge and gazing out of the window at a train just gliding into the station.

He seemed pensive and Vivienne started to feel slightly uneasy. She knew Steven so well.

"Well, Steven, let's hear about your trip … how did you find Paris?"

Steven was drinking his coffee and seemed to be taking his time. It was as if he needed to organize his thoughts and to say things in the right way. After all, thought Vivienne, he's been gone almost a week and a lot must have happened in that time.

A lot *had* happened, because Steven began slowly. "It's difficult to tell you, Mom, but I will be relocating to Paris. The interview went off superbly. The big boss likes me and wants me there, in his office." He looked at Vivienne to see how she was taking it.

The blood had drained from her face. This couldn't be happening! She felt sick. This bright spot in her early morning was not going to be here.

She managed to gasp out in a low voice, "For how long, Steven?"

Steven twirled the cup around in his hand. He looked down at the cup not seeming to want to meet Vivienne's distressed face.

"Don't take it badly Mom," he said. "It's part of my journey. It may not be for long." There was a hesitancy in his voice.

Vivienne's mind was swirling. *So much better here!* She had been here barely two weeks and would be alone in a village to which she felt no connection. None at all. How long would Steven be gone for? She persisted with her question.

"Steven, for how long will you be gone? I was depending on you helping me here." Then she added in an accusing tone, "You said you would be here for me."

Steven brindled at that. "Mom, I didn't know this would happen. I can hardly say no."

"But you haven't answered me, Steven. For how long?"

Steven drew a deep breath. "Mom, for a couple of weeks to start with." Then seeming to feel he needed to say it, "Though it might be permanent."

Vivienne's face flushed from white to red. She was feeling angry now. "You can't know how I feel, Steven," she said. "I know no one here."

Steven was building up courage and replied, "Mom, you'll soon see how friendly the people are. You know you were in a rut in Cowies Hill."

At this, Vivienne felt her anger rising. "Steven I was settled there. It might not have been exciting, but I knew people. I liked

73

the house. Even though I bought it after your father's death I was very happy in it on my own. "

"Dad passed away twenty years ago," said Steven. "You are still young. You could start a new life here, Mom."

"Really Steven? How can you say such a thing? My life was fine. I don't want a new life as you call it. In fact, I don't know what to do with my time."

She really felt she was about to burst into tears. What a let-down!

"Mom, there are lots of activities here. Book clubs, a theatre with plays and a garden club."

Vivienne snorted. "But I don't have a garden. Back at Cowies Hill I had one and was happy in the garden club."

Steven was not wanting to argue or discuss further, Vivienne could see by the way he kept silent and just shrugged his shoulders. That made her even angrier.

"You don't seem to care, Steven," she said. "I was so happy to be near you, that's why I sold up." It wasn't only that, she knew, but it seemed the thing that Steven needed to hear.

He took a deep breath. "Mom, I can't do anything about what is happening. I will shop for you and get you everything you want or need so you are well stocked up. And you really have everything you need here." He pointed to the view outside of a shining sea with a sun gleaming on its <u>surface</u>. "You're next to the sea, with a lovely view. And this is a lovely house. It is central and well-equipped."

He was defending his choices now, Vivienne knew that and his encouragement of her to come here.

"You told me it was so much better here," she said bitterly. "I don't think that at all. I miss my friends. I miss the house and I miss my maid and I have no idea of what to do with my time." She thumped the small table next to her with sudden vehemence.

Steven looked shocked. He shook his head and stood up. "Mom, I'm going now. I'll call later when you are feeling better."

This only angered Vivienne more, but there was nothing she could do as Steven had stood up, picked up his coffee cup and plate, and walked with them to the kitchen. Vivienne sat, her head in her hands, taking in the news. She heard the back door shut and knew that Steven had gone.

Of course, she had only made the situation worse by reacting the way she had. She realised that now. She heard Steven's car pull out of his garage and felt as if her world had ended. She sat for a very long time, feeling morose and alone. Outside was the street she had walked in, that went past the jewellery shop and furniture shops and an art gallery and an ice cream parlour. She thought about it. Nothing interested her. May as well explore part s of the village she hadn't seen yet.

She couldn't sit indoors all day. She had done housework yesterday and had not moved. Today, she needed to walk and to walk quickly, anywhere. She first saw she had sensible walking shoes on and a hat, picked up her big floppy shopping bag with her sketch pad and pen.

She went down the large stairs from her front door past the café and glared at a man eating a hamburger, who smiled at her. She passed a woman with a baby in a pram and a young boy on a skate board. She crossed the road and was soon in another small twisty lane with large trees bordering the sidewalks. She walked a long way and began to feel hot and thirsty. Was there perhaps a café or tea room where she could purchase a cool drink? But the street looked more of a settled neighborhood with houses and no shops. She didn't want to get lost. Turning a corner, she bumped unexpectedly into a large man. Steadying herself, she looked up to apologize and saw a face she would know anywhere. The bearded face of Ivor.

"Whoa," he said. "You in a hurry?"

Vivienne halted. She was still in a bad mood, but the fast walking uphill had her panting for breath.

"Just looking for a tearoom to get a cold drink," she said. She wiped her forehead.

She saw Ivor looking at her quizzically. "Too nice a day to be rushing," he said, giving a faint smile that disappeared into his beard.

Vivienne hadn't noticed that it was a nice day. The desire to just walk, fast, anywhere, had taken away any notion of what the day was like.

"You won't find a tearoom here," said Ivor. Then he hesitated before adding, "but behind me is my house, if you would like to come in, I have cold drink in my fridge."

Vivienne was about to reject the offer when her strong feeling of needing a glass of water at least overtook her. She didn't actually smile, but at least she didn't glare at him as she had at the man in the café.

"Thank you," she said. "I really need just a drink of water."

Ivor had turned to open a small wooden gate. As she entered, the fragrance of jasmine was heavy in the air. She looked around and saw a heathy jasmine plant entwined and climbing a big old tree. Ivor saw her eyes on it.

He smiled into his beard. "Very strong scent it has, but I enjoy colours and smells. Being an artist, that's not surprising."

Vivienne was following him the short distance to his front door. She wondered if he had a wife and what she would say to him bringing her into the house.

As if he knew what she was thinking he said, "I live alone. That is best for an artist as I have very strange hours when I paint. Middle of the night sometimes."

He opened the front door and led Vivienne inside. She looked in amazement. His lounge wasn't a lounge in the normal sense of the word. It was as much a gallery as any gallery of paintings was. He had a variety of scenes all framed and standing on easels.

"I supply several art galleries, not just the coffee shop with the painting of the fisherman's cottage."

Vivienne looked around, amazed.

Ivor said, "But you didn't come here to look at my art. You came here for a drink of water. Perhaps you'd like to sit on my porch whilst I bring it to you? Water or cool drink?"

"Just water thanks," said Vivienne. She was already feeling cooler. Calmer even. She sighed.

Ivor looked at her. "You seemed distressed when I saw you," he said. "Anything wrong?"

Plenty was wrong, but Vivienne didn't feel like sharing this with this man. So she shook her head.

"Nothing I can't handle," she said.

Ivor disappeared into his kitchen to fetch her a glass of water. Vivienne had time to look around. Everything was neat and tidy. Pictures on the nicely painted pale goldy-pink walls.

"Good lighting for paintings," he said, returning with the water, then he added, "How did your time go with that witch who lives in that fisherman's cottage?"

"She's not a witch," defended Vivienne.

"Folks say she is," said Ivor, "which is why I didn't want to go inside."

Ivor set the water down on a small table next to Vivienne. He also had a small cake on a plate for her. She was touched by his thoughtfulness. Such a gruff-looking man, she thought, but maybe I misjudged him.

Ivor had settled himself in a chair opposite Vivienne. The porch led off the lounge and had long glass windows. It was edged with flowering pot plants. Vivienne's eyes were on the plants with their brightly coloured flowers. She saw Ivor watching her and wasn't surprised when he pointed to the plants.

"They are my children and I spend a lot of time looking after them."

"Yes," said Vivienne. "I can see they are strong and healthy."

"Indoor gardening, yes. Outside, it's a different story."

The outside garden was full of flowers, as well, but Vivienne could see that they were left to do as they pleased. The result was colorful, but chaotic and she smiled. "Everything looks happy doing as they please," she said.

Ivor had brought himself a glass of cold drink and a small cake which he began to eat. So Vivienne joined in, drinking the water first, because all that uphill walking at speed had drained her energy. The cake had the taste of almond in it. "Very nice, thank you," she said formally.

"I buy them in bulk and freeze them," offered Ivor. "I like to nibble when I create … think of what to paint, for instance. A lot of my work is creative watercolour, but I won't talk art as you probably aren't interested."

Suddenly Vivienne was. This was something she knew nothing about. And what else had she to do today?

She spoke. "If I am not upsetting your morning, Ivor, I'd love to see your creative watercolours, as it is something I know nothing about."

Ivor was drinking his coke, his cake finished. Vivienne had the feeling she needed to speed up as he was probably eager to show her and then get on with his day.

"I wasn't doing anything important," he said. "I sometimes go for a walk, just anywhere, before I start painting. Just to get my mind into idle. Into a space of no thought."

"Interesting," said Vivienne, who couldn't imagine having a no-thought head, though possibly this is what Lady Lavender was telling her.

"Yes, I like to paint without thinking," said Ivor.

Vivienne looked at him quizzically and he laughed.

"When I think, I spoil my paintings," he said. "I know where my colours are on my palette and my brush just goes into the colour that it wants to use next."

This sounded more odd than anything Vivienne had ever heard.

"I'll show you," said Ivor, getting up, obviously enthused with his art. He went into a small room off the lounge and brought out a large white palette covered in blobs of different-coloured paints.

"Yellow, red, blue, green dark brown and black. That's all I need," said Ivor. "I mix as I go and no two of my paintings are ever the same. The colours mix themselves, especially with wet-into-wet painting."

This was a new field for Vivienne, but she was interested and looked at the messy palette. She shook her head.

"How can you ever know where the colours are?" she asked.

"I don't know," he said. "That would be thinking and I don't think. The brush knows where the colours are and it is all really out of my hands. I just use the brush and dip it into paints as I feel urged to do."

Vivienne had finished her cake and had drunk her water. She stood up.

"Thank you," she said. "I feel a whole lot better now." And she actually smiled. Because she did. Surprisingly, a lot better.

"Please show me your paintings," she said.

Ivor picked up both glasses and plates and took them through to his kitchen. When he came out, he indicated to Vivienne to follow him into his lounge, where there were at least fifteen large paintings all framed and all different.

Some were very precise. His flower paintings were a mixture of loose creativity and exquisite tiny strokes as he painted the stamens of a flowering peach blossom. His roses were shaded and as real as any rose one could see growing in a garden.

But it was when it came to his large landscapes, done in what he called creative watercolours and using a wet-into-wet technique, where misty trees loomed out of deep crevices and white clouds hovered over fields of green grass with yellow and red flowers growing in profusion that he excelled. Or misty distant pale-mauve mountains with strong rough rocks in the foreground and young vibrant trees demanding to be noticed. His use of colour was eye-catching. Sudden little gleams of yellow on a dark landscape caught the eye. Reflections on rivers and lakes were beautiful.

"You must spend a lot of time painting," said Vivienne with deep respect.

"Oh, I do," said Ivor. "It is my life. And walking and seeing light and shadow, trees in summer and the autumn with leaves dropping and the stark bare trunks against a blue winter sky pleases my artist's soul."

"Then don't let me hold you up," said Vivienne, rested and ready to walk some more.

"As I said, I wasn't going anywhere in particular. Just walking where the mood took me. I often stumble on wonderful subjects to paint … " Then he added, looking at Vivienne, "Like old farm buildings and small wooden sheds. You might like to sketch them too." Then he added, "Would you like to come on my walk with me?"

Vivienne could never have seen her doing this a week or so ago when she first went into that coffee shop and Ivor spoke to her. She had been quite brusque in wanting to get rid of him. Now here she was about to agree to walk with him and to sketch farm buildings somewhere.

"It is off the beaten track as it were, one goes towards the mountains and at the base there is this old shed, very artistic, as I see it. Come with me."

He stood up, picked up a small sling bag and indicated to Vivienne to go out, whilst he locked up. Soon they were in the street outside of his small wooden gate and he was pointing upwards. "See that mountain in the distance." Vivienne could see it beyond the houses, a humpy kind of mountain with white rocks and a lot of green bushy trees.

"We don't go nearly as far, but at the start of the open land there is this old farm building. I'm glad you have strong walking shoes on." He looked at her in a kindly way and Vivienne felt a warmth she hadn't felt for days. Especially not since Steven had started talking of Paris.

Steven! Even as she hurried to keep up with the long strides of Ivor as he led her down a back street then up towards the base of the mountain, Steven flew into her mind. She wouldn't be hot and walking uphill with this strange man if Steven had behaved as she had expected him to. This sudden need to oblige his work boss upset Vivienne a lot. No doubt, Mariette had a lot to do with it. She tripped over a clump of grass and steadied herself as Ivor turned to say, "Are you alright? Am I walking too fast?"

"No," said Vivienne untruthfully. "I wasn't looking where I was going, but I'm okay."

Ivor nodded his head, looked at Vivienne with piercing hazel eyes that seemed to show he didn't quite believe her. He smiled gently. "I'll walk slower so you have time to see where we are going."

Where they were going was up a steep path that wound and became very narrow. Then the tar tapered off and they were walking on soft crunchy green grass.

"This feels much better," said Vivienne, panting slightly.

"Oh yes, the grass is part of Mother Earth," said Ivor easily.

He had slowed right down and Vivienne caught up to him. He stopped and pointed. "See there over to the right, you can catch a glimpse of the roof of the building we are going to sketch."

They walked on over the lumpy green grass, Vivienne now beside Ivor as the path was non-existent. He was a large man, large in every way, she thought. There was a turn around the trees and the old barn was right in front of them. The sun was shining down on the roof and the rickety wooden planks that it was made of were rotten in parts and creepers peeped through. There was an old door with a padlock on it, and a window that was dull with dust. But it did have a charm about it.

"Funny that old disused barns and sheds fascinate artists," Vivienne said. "I have seen other pictures of old barns."

"I suppose they tell a story of their own," said Ivor. "If you use your imagination, you may wonder who found this shed valuable. And kept it locked. What was it used for? Why build it here? The imagination can build a whole story around it."

"Much like the fisherman's cottage," said Vivienne.

"Yes, I have often wondered about the people who lived there and how they came to such an isolated place. Were they shipwrecked? Did they come from lands far away?"

"I was hoping to find out those things from Lady Lavender, as I call her, because of the lavender she has growing…"

"And you didn't?" asked Ivor.

Vivienne sighed. "No," she said slowly. "The conversation didn't go that way."

Ivor laughed. "Conversations often go where they are meant to go.. and right now, our conversation stops as you and I have to give our attention to this old beauty." He said it with such affection that Vivienne took another look at the old barn.

From around a corner the ginger face of a cat appeared. "Well, someone else likes it here," she said, pointing to the cat which had jumped up and found a broken plank with a gap big enough for the cat to squeeze through.

"I guess there are mice inside," said Ivor.

Vivienne remembered her lesson in art. Only draw what you find interesting. She nodded to Ivor who had taken out a sketch book and a palette of colours, along with a brush in a small bottle of water.

"I'll sketch and paint as I go," he said.

Vivienne didn't feel like standing to sketch so she looked around and found a bendy tree on which she could sit. She opened her sling bag and took out her sketch book and drew the door with the broken pane.

"Yes, that's a story in itself," said Vivienne.

What did she like about this cottage? Perhaps the part with the door and the broken panel into which the cat had jumped. Obligingly, at that moment, the ginger face of the cat reappeared with a wriggling mouse in its mouth. Vivienne wanted to make the cat drop the mouse so that it had its chance to live, but thought better of it. The cat hesitated just long enough for Vivienne to do a quick outline of the cat's face before it jumped down. In the process, the mouse escaped and ran off into the grass.

"Life is always interesting," said Ivor, who had been watching the whole performance.

He didn't look to see what Vivienne was drawing as he was busy himself.

Both finished their sketches within minutes of each other. Then Ivor ws interested to see Vivienne's work.

He looked at it quizzically then spoke. "I like it," he said. "You definitely have talent."

"I've never thought of it," said Vivienne. "This is just a very spare-time hobby of mine and I've had no training. Just some suggestions given to me by an art teacher at a school my husband taught at."

Ivor showed her his line-and-wash drawing. He had drawn the whole barn, with the creeper peeping through a broken board. He had washed in colours, blue for the sky above, green for the creeper, a pinky-brown for the old shed, and he had indicated the mountain behind just with a few strokes.

"I can either leave it as it is, or use it to paint a larger picture when I get home," he said. "When I have a clear mind ..."

He smiled at Vivienne and suddenly Steven jumped into her mind again. Would she ever have a clear and empty mind that didn't think of Steven?

Their sketching session over, Ivor nodded to Vivienne, indicating that they would be going back. It was easier going downhill, but when they came to Ivor's cottage Vivienne declined an invitation to get anything to drink and thanked him most sincerely for his time that morning. She walked home slowly, her thoughts a muddle of sketching and disappointment with Steven. He had left so angrily this morning. What would his mood be like when next she saw him? It mattered more than it should.

Vivienne let herself in through the kitchen. She didn't want a confrontation with Steven, but she was pleased to look around her small kitchen with its counter beneath the window she opened each morning to attract Steven. She wondered now if she would ever make sense of her life.

Here she was in Kalk Bay where Steven told her it would be so much better. Right now, it wasn't. She missed her quiet house in Cowies Hill with her spacious garden and the occasional wave from a neighbour. She missed her pattern of life with the weekly visits, one at a time, from Jenny, Muriel and critical Henriette.... All different. All adding something to her life. But she knew she wasn't ready to phone any of them, not until she had positive proof that it was definitely better for her in Kalk Bay.

Steven had been such an attraction to her. Her only son who had been such a rock after Paul's death. Steven had been a teenager, but had taken on the role of the man in the house and learnt to fix things and generally help her where he could. She, in her turn, had helped Steven all she could, encouraged him to learn to drive, to use her car until he could afford one of his own. She had encouraged his development into internet marketing and had triumphed with him as he grew in ability and eventually was offered this job in Capetown. That was a year ago and they had kept in frequent touch, mostly on her side, but with brief and she realised it now, superficial messages from Steven.

In their thirty-five years since he was born, they had never had a serious fall-out. Not like this morning where he had walked out on her. Would he call in this evening? Would he come over for coffee tomorrow morning? The thoughts haunted her. She didn't usually make coffee at night, but if she did and the strong aroma wafted across the narrow lane, it might bring him over.

She wasn't hungry, so she settled for a simple meal of salads and tuna, and instead made the filter pot of strong coffee. If he wanted supper, she could easily make something for him, but the coffee was what she was hoping would attract him.

It was extra strong and a small wind blowing the right way was sure to take over the aroma to him. *Would he respond?* She hoped so much that he would. It was nerve-wracking to sit in the kitchen and wait. But there was no action from across the lane. In the end, she left the windows open and the coffee pot simmering on the stove and went to the lounge. *What to do now?* Her mind was filled with despairing thoughts. This small lounge overlooked the station in the distance and the café downstairs. They brought all those people. She realised she didn't really like people. Not crowds of people, all milling around and chatting. Not to her, but to each other.

Vivienne spent a gloomy night alone, and later, closed the kitchen windows and took the coffee off the stove. By now, it had almost simmered away. She looked at it sadly and tipped what remained into the rubbish bin. Maybe tomorrow would be better.

Chapter 6

The dawn was astounding. Reds and rose-pinks, mixed with deep golds and brilliant sunshine yellow, all exploding from a deep navy sky. If she could paint, she would never be able to capture this splendour. She thought of Ivor. And wondered, had he ever painted sunrises or sunsets? If she could paint, what would she love to do? Just paint the sky. Didn't the sky change eternally? Cloudy blue skies with no hint of rain, stormy skies, beautiful sunsets that she couldn't see from the east coast of Cape Town, but which she knew were amazing and then, of course, these amazing dawns. That filled her soul with good thoughts. So she showered and got dressed.

She had suffered such insecurities the last twenty-four hours and she knew she needed Steven, so, as usual, she went through to make the coffee. Would Steven come over? Surely, he wasn't so angry with her that he would stop those early morning visits? And how much longer was she likely to enjoy them? Mariette and Paris were annoying realities.

To her abounding pleasure, at the usual time came the sound of the door opposite her opening, and then closing, followed by the sound of quick footsteps across the cobbled lane. Then the sound of Steven's voice, steady and normal, as he knocked and called as he opened the door, "Morning, Mom." He was cautious and serious in his approach, as if he wasn't sure of his welcome.

But Vivienne's relief at seeing him was so great that she positively beamed and held out her arms to hug Steven, who seemed a bit taken aback. She was normally not demonstrative. However, she had such a terrible time in her mind for the past twenty-four hours that peace between them was all that she wanted for now.

No point digging up anything controversial so she simply said, "Ready for a strong cup of coffee, Steven?"

Steven smiled with a look of relief on his face. "Absolutely. Thanks, Mom."

Vivienne placed a large steaming mug of aromatic coffee next to Steven as he sat on a bar stool in her kitchen. Neither said anything. Instead, he cautiously lifted the coffee to his mouth. He seemed to test it but stopped.

"It's piping hot, Mom," he said.

Vivienne said nothing. Whatever she might say could be the wrong thing so rather not talk at all.

Steven looked at her doubtfully. "You okay, Mom? You are very quiet."

Vivienne wasn't sure if she was okay or not. There was so much to ask him, so much to say, but also it could lead to arguments.

So she simply said, "Yes I'm okay, but I would like to hear about your next move." There it was out, her biggest worry...*What was Steven going to do and when?*

Steven looked relieved. "I'm glad you are okay, Mom," he said. "It really is the best seaside village you could ever find."

Vivienne kept quiet. This she didn't need to hear. What she did want to hear was about his move to Paris, and a worry that Mariette might be playing a big part in his life. She spoke. "I'm talking about your move to Paris."

"Oh, that," Steven said casually as if it was an afterthought. "It will happen soon. Very soon."

Viviene breathed deeply. This was bad news. She wanted badly to know about Mariette so she took another deep breath. "And Mariette?"

"Oh yes," said Steven in a carefully casual way. "She will be there. Her father is the big boss."

"Where will you stay?"

Steven took another deep breath. Then he looked defensively at Vivienne. "

They like me," he said, "so her mother asked if I would like to stay with them. Their apartment is very close to her father's business so he just walks to work and so will I."

Vivenne was horrified. What was to happen to her? Did Steven even think of that?

"Oh, Steven I like you too," Vivienne almost wailed. "I moved here because of you and because you said it was so much better here."

Steven became defensive. "Mom, I didn't know any of this would happen."

"But you could have said NO."

"And lose my chance of a possible partnership, Mom? Think what I will be able to do for you with a much-increased income."

"It's not the material things, Steven," said Vivienne. "It's your presence I like … I need."

Vivienne could see that Steven was having a hard time to keep calm. He was breathing heavily.

"I never imagined you would take it this way," he said. "You have plenty of money with the sale of the house. You are living in this friendly seaside village where it is so safe. I worried about you in Cowies Hill with all the robberies."

Vivienne could feel herself getting angry. But if she said how she was really feeling, Steven would probably walk out as he did yesterday morning. So she bit her tongue and instead of an angry retort, she said rather sadly, "Steven, I enjoyed my life in Cowies Hill."

"You never did anything interesting, not since you retired," said Steven. "What did you do and where did you go that's stimulating?"

"I don't need stimulating, Steven. I had friends."

"Those three crazy women? Compare them with here… art galleries, music in the street and in concerts, a theatre, creative people and the sea and the fish. It's a paradise, Mom, if you just stopped to think."

Vivienne was close to tears. She never cried, but inside, she was weeping buckets. Steven seemed unaware of the pain all this was causing her.

Steven put down his coffee cup and stood up. Vivienne could see the visit was nearly over. Quickly she said, "Can I make you supper tonight, or perhaps we can eat out?"

"Mom I don't think so. I have Mariette to look after."

"Mariette. You only met her two weeks ago. She must be able to manage on her own by now. I need you, Steven, especially if I am not going to be seeing you for a long time."

"Mom, we'll make a nice evening of it, all three of us together. Maybe tomorrow night. I will be leaving the day after tomorrow."

He was standing up now and looking steadily at her. "Mom, I think I'm in love with Mariette," he said.

Vivienne nearly choked. All this so quickly! And she said, "How can you say that, Steven?"

"Mom, I know what I want and I've been hoping to meet someone someday exactly like Mariette. You must know that some day I'd meet someone and marry her."

"Yes," said Vivienne, "I suppose so, but I always imagined I'd be close to you, to be part of your life still, but with you going to Paris …" Her face crumpled and Steven came over and put his arms round her.

"You are the best mom in the world," he said. "I know what you've done for me. But I have my whole life to live. You had yours with dad, Mom, and you were very happy."

Vivienne choked back her deep feelings. Saying the wrong thing might cause her to lose him forever.

So she said nothing, but shook her head. Steven stood back and looked at her.

"It will all be fine, Mom," he said. "You'll find that it *is* much better here, and I'll always keep in touch."

He looked at her gravely. "Mom, you'll always matter to me," he said, "but I have to do what I have to do."

Vivienne looked at her son. Tall and kind and always so helpful. She loved him deeply, but what could she do about this situation? Nothing, she realised. With an unsteady voice she said, "It will be nice to have dinner with you both."

At this, he nodded, turned, and went out of the kitchen door, closing it very quietly after him.

Vivienne flopped down onto a kitchen chair. This was the worst news she had had in a long time. *How to digest it?* She shook her head. She sat for quite a long time, thoughts churning in her head. Steven, in love with Mariette, going to live in Paris and staying with his boss. Living in Paris probably. And her, not in her own peaceful house in Cowies Hill, but here in a small house in a busy seaside village teeming with residents she didn't know and with visitors she didn't know either. She had time on her hands and certainly money, but what use was money when what she really wanted was her son to be part of her life.

And here she was alone in Kalk Bay.

Should she phone one of her friends? But she would have to tell them this devastating news and they would just tell her they told her she was being stupid. What to do with her time? Perhaps go and sit on one of those chairs under the umbrellas and look at the sea. But no, there would be happy laughing people and she was not happy or laughing. Seeing people in high good spirits would just depress her more.

Some instinct suggested a visit to Lady Lavender. It would not be a jolly visit where they sat and laughed, but it was someone to talk to. And she needed an ear most desperately. There could be a baby in time and she wouldn't be there. This thought upset her even more. On a sudden whim, she went outside, locked her front door, went down the steps past the café and hurried along the road. She bumped into a pole, steadied herself and reminded herself that Lady Lavender was the one who had said she only had this moment to live in and that she needed to enjoy it. She certainly was missing something. She was still upset when she reached the fisherman's cottage and knocked on the door.

It was opened immediately by Lady Lavender with her large black cat beside her. Today, she had on a long skirt patterned in navy and white with a navy top. She looked impressive. Vivienne looked at her deep-set all seeing eyes and flushed as Lady Lavender said, "I've been expecting you."

"But I didn't know I was coming until about an hour ago," said Vivienne.

"All the same, I've been expecting you, Vivienne. Please come in. Shall we go to the kitchen and get ourselves a cup of ginger tea and this time the biscuits are almond-flavoured."

Vivienne saw her looking at Vivienne in a kindly way and felt a great wave of relief flood over her. Lady Lavender couldn't be called a friend, but Vivienne felt she could trust her maybe just to listen… Vivienne felt confused and even a bit afraid.

"Nice weather today," said Lady Lavender, looking at Vivienne.

"I hadn't noticed," said Vivienne without thinking.

Lady lavender smiled. "We spoke last time about being in the moment, if you remember, Vivienne."

Vivienne did but that didn't help her state of mind right now.

"What is it my dear? What is troubling you so badly?" asked Lady lavender.

Vivienne had the oddest feeling that she knew what was troubling her but wanted Vivienne to spell it out.

"It's my son, Lady Lavender."

"The one you kept thinking about the last time you were here?"

"Yes, that son."

"What has he done?"

"Nothing yet. But in two days' time he's going to Paris to live."

Lady Lavender looked quizzically at Vivienne waiting for her to say more.

"The only reason I sold my house and came to Kalk Bay was to be near to him," said Vivienne indignantly.

"Whoa... steady," said Lady Lavender. "Things aren't always about ourselves."

"I know," said Vivienne, now not afraid to talk. "I realise he has his own life to live, but... Lady Lavender, he says he's in love with this girl and I see him marrying her and living permanently in Paris."

"Who are you thinking about, Vivienne? Them ... or yourself?"

Vivienne hesitated. "I'm thinking about myself," she said slowly.

"Of course, you are. Take a step back and think about your son and this young lady. Are you not happy for them?"

Vivienne had to be honest.

"No," she said. "Everything was fine until she showed up. I wouldn't have sold up and left my home if I'd known this was to happen."

"Vivienne, accept that it has happened. You have sold your house and you have moved here. You will feel better if you find things to be grateful for that are here. Because regretting anything is not going to bring it back. This really is the only thing you have. This moment. And all the 'this moment's' make up your life. Happy or otherwise. Your choice."

Again, this wasn't the kind of conversation Vivienne was hoping to have. But all the same Lady Lavender's voice had a calming effect on Vivienne.

"How can I be happy when the thing I came to Kalk Bay for, to be close to my son, is not going to happen?" she said. She felt better for saying it.

"It's the way you look at it, Vivienne," said Lady Lavender. "This is the only moment you have for a happy life. You make it either way, by the way you think."

"It's the only thing that's in my mind," said Vivienne.

"Then swivel your mind in another direction Vivienne. Unclutter your mind. Keep it still and peaceful."

Vivienne had an urge to slam her fist on the table beside her. She didn't need a lecture. She needed an ear to listen to her woes.

"No, Vivienne, they aren't your woes. You are making them your woes."

Irritating woman, how did she know what I was thinking?

"Stay in the moment, Vivienne. I'll wait."

Vivienne didn't like being lectured to, but she was in despair. Slowly, she looked around d the room. At the fireplace with its cobbled stone around it, with the small windows with black wooden frames, at the view outside. She could just glimpse the bay and she could see the old tree she sat on the other day. She took some deep breaths and did her best to observe where she was. Lady Lavender's lounge was quite sparsely decorated, but had a big comfy sofa that Lady Lavender was sitting on and two large comfy armchairs, one of which Vivienne was occupying.

Suddenly, with blinding clarity, she saw the mess her mind was in. Time to slow down, to regain her quiet centre, to stop obsessing about what she could do nothing about.

"But, Lady Lavender, I have come to a strange village where I don't know anyone, where I don't have things to occupy my mind, as I did back in Cowies Hill. It would have been all right if Steven was staying here, but he is leaving for overseas and I am alone here."

"There is nothing that happens by chance," said Lady Lavender. "You were meant to come here. That is the first thing you have to accept."

"I don't want to think that way," objected Vivienne.

"If you want a happy peaceful life, you are going to need to change the way you think, Vivienne. Think of the young couple. You have had your life and your happiness, doing what you wanted to do. Your son is doing the same thing."

Vivienne sighed. "Yes, but if I'd known, I wouldn't have moved."

"You didn't know and you did move. Accept those facts, Vivienne. Then start from there. Meantime, your ginger tea is getting cold … and how do you like my almond biscuits?"

Vivienne watched her mind now, watched it swivel from her thoughts of Steven and Mariette to the almond biscuit. She thought only of the almond biscuit and slowly bit into it. Like the biscuits she had had here last time, the pastry was soft and buttery with a strong flavour of almond. She tried staying in the moment and savouring the biscuit as it melted in her mouth and then she watched herself swallowing it. Suddenly, she smiled. And Lady Lavender smiled too.

"Back in the moment, Vivienne?" she asked. "And enjoying it."

It was true … she had thought only of the biscuit and not of Steven and her lonely plight.

"There, doesn't that feel better," said Lady Lavender. "And do drink your tea whilst it is hot."

Vivienne obligingly held the delicate china cup to her lips and took a sip. Again, she thought only of drinking the ginger tea, of the taste of ginger with the sweet additional flavour of honey. She sighed. Yes, at this moment, she was in the moment, in a cottage with Lady Lavender and her head was not filled with despairing thoughts of Steven.

"Disciplining one's mind is like breaking in a wild horse," said Lady Lavender. "One has to be gentle with it. Be kind. When it strays, just bring it back gently to the present moment. If you make a habit of this you will find you can easily cope with your son's transfer overseas."

Vivienne shook her head. At this moment, she didn't believe Lady Lavender. Her mind would be constantly thinking of Steven she knew that.

"Just train your mind to stay in the moment, Vivienne. Don't let it wander all over the place. Consider your blessings. You have a house I take it."

"Yes, I do."

"And food and a bed."

"Yes, all of that."

"Those alone are blessings. Stay conscious of everything you do. Be aware of making your breakfast, of running water into your bath, of walking down the street. Keep your attention onto exactly what you are doing. Don't let other thoughts intrude. You will see an improvement in how you feel."

Vivienne looked at Lady Lavender and sighed.

"Yes, it's much easier to be miserable and to feed your ego," said Lady Lavender, "but peace doesn't come that way. It comes from being grateful for what you have, for this lovely day, for the blue sky and the birds, the sea out there and all life around. We live in an abundant world, Vivienne, and abundant blessings await you when you have learned to train that mind of yours."

Vivienne opened her mouth to speak, but closed it again. She was watching her thoughts. She had never really done this before and she was finding an amazing thing happening. Her head was becoming quiet and peaceful.

She signed.

"Thank you, Lady Lavender," she said. "Something deep inside me made me come to you today. I was in a bad state."

"Now keep out of that bad state, Vivienne, and learn to enjoy each moment. They all have value and add up to make a happy life. Before you leave, please close your eyes and just watch what you are thinking. Catch a thought and watch it. Just watch it...." Her voice tailed off. "Keep your eyes shut, Vivienne, and tell me what is in your mind right now."

Vivienne, with her eyes shut, said in surprise, "Nothing."

"Excellent," said Lady Lavender, "and from that nothing I would like you to imagine peace, silence, abundance, ,joy, bliss ... something like that and to stay in that silent frame of mind in a joyous or silent state. If you learn to do this, Vivienne, you will know peace ... peace in any circumstance ... and, thank you, when you are ready, you may open your eyes."

Vivienne opened them and sat in silence looking at Lady Lavender. She had a peaceful head and knew a silence inside her she had never known.

She looked at the enigmatic mysterious woman and just shook her head. Lady Lavender gave her a lovely smile.

"You've had a great lesson today, Vivienne. Do your best to remember it. And go in peace!"

Walking back up the hill, Vivienne remembered to keep her attention on what she was doing. Walking. She watched the path ahead and on both sides, and noticed trees she hadn't seen on her way to lady lavender. The sky was a deep blue with sunlight glancing off the leaves of the trees. Vivienne was puffing slightly by the time she reached the main road and found her way home. She looked at the cobbled lane as she walked up it and to her back door. She had never really looked at the slightly different colours of the slates and of their slight shine. The back door of her house was also one she had not really looked at before. Now she noticed that it was painted green and had a welcome sign she had never really seen before. She grimaced. She was going to be kept busy just staying in the moment!

Chapter 7

Dinner with Steven and Mariette was a success. Vivienne watched herself carefully to see she didn't make any irreversible errors in how she treated Mariette. She was charming and reserved, and let the young couple chatter away. Mariette seemed much more relaxed and Vivienne was keenly aware of how Steven looked at her and how he treated her. After all, his happiness was what she said she always wanted for him.

Steven was relaxed and as he saw Vivienne into her home via the kitchen, he said, "I'll see you for coffee tomorrow morning, Mom, then I won't be seeing you for quite a while." He looked at her with a serious face then kissed her lightly on the cheek. "Thanks Mom, see you tomorrow." And he was gone…

Vivienne did her best to remember that the evening was over, Steven had gone and she was in her new home. It was difficult and she sighed. Then she caught site of an unwashed cup and put all her attention on to squirting it with dishwasher, then running the hot water tap into it and washing the coffee stains off the inside. Just watch what I am doing and think of nothing else, she told herself. It wasn't easy but it did lead to a peaceful and easy sleep for which she was grateful.

Vivienne awoke and greeted the dawn as she always did. She noticed that she wanted to think about Steven visiting for coffee, but pulled her thoughts back into looking at the dark sky with its pinpricks of stars. She was up before dawn today and had a determination to stay in the moment, looking at the sky. When would she see the first glimmer of the sun? She continued to watch the sky with its pinpricks of stars. How she had wished upon a star as a small child. Now she was wishing upon a star for some sense in her life, some feeling of everything being as it should, but inherently, she knew that it wasn't .. not right now. Back to looking at the sky, stop thinking, she told herself.

At that moment she saw the first faint rays of gold creep through the blanket of navy blue. It was followed by some rays of red then, quite suddenly, by a whole host of glorious reds, golds and yellows; she watched, breathless almost. It all happened so quickly and then with a triumphant blast, the sun itself arrived, big and reddish-golden, instantly clearing away the navy of night, replacing it with golds and yellows and above it all, a blue sky... such a magical moment and Vivienne's heart lifted. To stay in this joyous state all day would be so marvellous!

She stayed a little longer, looking now at a golden day with a blue sky, before going off to shower, get dressed and to put on the coffee. Today, she would add cream to the coffee and make the best cup of coffee she had ever made.

In no time at all, the windows were open, and the strong aroma of coffee was filling the air. Vivienne got out two special mugs, the cream and, for her, the sugar. Steven didn't sweeten his coffee, preferring the flavour of strong coffee.

All was ready when she heard the door opposite her open and then the sound of quick footsteps across the cobbled lane. Then the quick knock on the door, then Steven appeared.

He looked excited. How could she dampen this excitement? It was his opportunity to fly to new heights with a pretty girl at his side. Lucky, it was a small intimate firm where they didn't seem to mind personal relationships within the business. She decided to say nothing. To let Steven talk.

"Coffee ready, Mom?" he asked.

"And there's cream to go in it today," said Vivienne with a small smile. "Let's enjoy the coffee and you being here with me," she said. Then with quiet confidence, she added, "It's all going to be fine, Steven."

At that he relaxed. "Really Mom? You are happy with being here by yourself?"

Vivienne thought to herself, I wouldn't call it happy, but she decided not to air her thoughts.

"I'll be fine, thanks, Steven," she said. "It's you who is making your mark on life. Making your dreams come true. I'm happy about you and Mariette." She wasn't really, but from Steven's point of view she was.

Steven smiled and gave her a big hug. "That's the best news, Mom. I worried about how you would feel about a soon-to-be daughter in law... you will come over to Paris for the wedding, won't you? In about six months' time."

Vivienne nodded her head. "Of course, Steven. Thank you."

"You'll love all the pavement artists and the small roadside cafes and the night life. And the trees beside the Seine River."

Vivienne smiled at his enthusiasm. "You'll need to learn how to speak French, Steven."

"Oh, I'm already brushing up on that, Mom, Steven said. "So much that is new and exciting. And yes, I won't be seeing you for a while. But we can always Zoom and chat, so I'll be in touch."

Vivienne knew at that moment that he would stay in touch and really talk to her.. . simply by accepting the moment and his decisions. To get it right. Steven put down his coffee cup.

"That was the best coffee I've ever had," he said. He stood up. "Time for me to be going now, Mom," he said.

"Let me give you an *au revoir* hug." Vivienne stood up. Her heart was full of joy and sadness and much else, but she enjoyed Steven's hug, the smell of his aftershave and the faint odour that she always associated with Steven. Then he kissed her again and was gone. Shortly after that, she heard the garage door across the way opening and saw the white car drawing out, the garage gates closing and the car driving off.

What had Lady Lavender told her? That she had only this moment, that she needed to be in that moment and aware, and not let her mind drift. It badly wanted to with the knowledge that that was the last she would see of Steven for goodness knows how long. Just the thought of that made her want to shrivel up and die. No, not yet, go back to Cowies Hill. But there would be no going back. There was just this moment and she was here, in a small house new to her in the village of Kalk Bay.

If I am in this moment then let me look around the kitchen and tidy it up after the coffee, she told herself resolutely and did her best to just concentrate on what she was doing. It wasn't easy, but she was managing. Then there came a thump at her window and she looked up startled, a bird had flown into it and had knocked its head.

Poor bird! Was it injured? She went out of the kitchen and down the steps. The bird, a bright yellow in colour, was lying on the cobbled road. She hurried over to it and gently picked it up. It was warm and soft and it was breathing. But its eyes were closed. Carrying it gently back into the kitchen, she stood holding it and wondering what to do. *Perhaps s sip of water?* Holding a teaspoon of water close to its beak, she let a few drops of water fall onto its beak. The bird shuddered, opened its beak and its eyes and flew off, straight at the window again. Could she catch it and let it go out of the window that was open? She picked up a soft dishcloth, and swiftly put it over the bird, then she picked up the wriggling bundle and let it go out of the open window. Then all she saw was a flash of bright yellow as the bird flew off.

Vivienne found her heart was pounding. So much drama, she

wasn't sure if it was seeing the last of Steven for goodness knows how long, or saving the bird.

She sat on a chair, breathing deeply. Then she reminded herself to stay focused, deal with the kitchen then decide what to do with the rest of the day. She realised that she had no plans for her life. No burning desire to do anything. No, she couldn't waste her life by walking around aimlessly.

A sudden flash came to her. What about visiting Ivor today and seeing if he could help her with some painting if he wasn't too busy? He had seemed welcoming when she had bumped into him a few days ago.

Her mind made up, she spent an hour cleaning and tidying up, then with a surprisingly light heart, she went out of her front door, down the five steps and past the busy customers at the café. This time when a man eating a hamburger smiled at her, she smiled back. No harm in that. Soon she was walking up the street, passing the now-familiar shops and remembering to be aware of what she was seeing and what she was thinking. This was all new and quite difficult.

She veered off into a side street, remembering the course she had taken when walking aimlessly and then bumping into Ivor. A few more bends, up a couple more blocks, round the corner and then there was the small wooden gate. She wondered if he would be in, or if he was out walking.

She looked at the leavy branches of a tree, noticed how the bark was shaded differently and smiled. Yes, she was in the moment. And would Ivor be in? There was a bell at the gate and she rang it.

She waited anxiously, but the door opened, and there stood Ivor in a kind of a smock that was covered in paint. He looked up at the gate and she knew he had seen her, because he smiled and waved, and made quick steps to get to the gate to open it.

'' Good morning, Vivienne," he said formally.

"Good morning, Ivor," she replied seriously.

He smiled at her. "Nice day, eh, Vivienne."

This time, Vivienne had observed the day as she had walked, as well as a lot of other details so she answered with a slight smile, "Yes, it is, Ivor."

"You looked deeply troubled the other day," said Ivor. "Today you look almost joyous."

"Thank you, Ivor. And I may be even more joyous if you are able to help me."

"With what Vivienne?"

"You were so kind to me last time I saw you, taking me out to sketch. But now ..." She hesitated.

"And now?" Ivor persisted.

"Now I wondered how busy you are... if you could show me how to put paint onto my small sketch or to paint something new."

Ivor hesitated as if considering his options. Then he said, "As you can see, I am in my studio and I am painting. I can give you a brush and one tube of paint and show you how to use the brush. I use big brushes called hakes. Then you can practice on a piece of paper I can also give you. How does that sound?"

Vivienne's heart lifted and she smiled. "Wonderful," she said. And she meant it.

Soon they were in the house in a room leading off the lounge with all the framed paintings and in a long very airy room with long windows and large tables with paintings laid out on them. Ivor cleared a painting off one of the tables and put a sheet of water-colour paper on it. He looked in a box of paints and came out with a tube of paint.

"It's called burnt umber," he said. "And here is a hake and a palette to work on, plus a jar of water to wet your brush. And an old piece of cloth to mop off excess water from your brush. I'll show you what this hake can do."

Vivienne looked at the flat ungainly brush. "It's so versatile," said Ivor, "it quickly puts down paint on big areas like skies or sea, and you can also move it sideways so it can paint a fine branch on a tree." And he proceeded to show Vivienne on another small piece of paper. "See, too, how the colour changes with the amount of water you use. When you first begin painting it is a good idea to learn to be able to work from light to dark and dark to light with just one colour. Later, you can add other colours and learn to mix them to get shades of colours that you want."

Vivienne suddenly knew what she wanted to paint. "Ivor, what I would really like to paint are sunrises. They are never the same. And they are so inspirational."

"Well, you have a starting point anyway," said Ivor. "Good, some practice with the burnt umber will give you the confidence to do a big wash of an early-morning sky, I guess before the sun rises."

Vivienne nodded. This was joy, indeed. She smiled at Ivor. She hadn't noticed what a sensitive face he had. Hidden in all that beard. How she had misjudged him that first time they had spoken! But so much had happened to her in the past week… it was as if she had passed through several lifetimes.

"Well," said Ivor, "you puddle away here, while I finish this river scene. I paint wet into wet which I can show you later but the wet needs me to paint into it now, or I will lose the effect of the reflections that I know I can get."

Soon, Vivienne had squirted a big blob of burnt umber onto her palette and had cautiously mixed in some water. She dampened the brush and made her first tentative brush stroke.

Ivor, watching her, smiled, "That's called dry scrumbling," he said. "When you want to paint something with highlights in it you use that technique. You need to add more water and then move the brush quickly across the whole width of the paper. That's called a wash. And its basic to painting. You need to get your washes perfect as they will be used for skies, rivers, distant fields, lakes and the sea. Don't' be scared. Just try it. It's just a piece of paper." He smiled into his beard.

Vivienne knew he wasn't smiling at her, but rather enjoying teaching her some of the elements of painting. She was glad he had turned back to his own painting and wasn't watching her as she put more water on her hake and mixed the paint on the palette until it was an even pale brown then, taking a big breath, she laid the brush flat on the paper and drew it rapidly across the paper.

Ivor was watching her out of the corner of his eye and he nodded. "Good stuff, Vivienne, Do another stroke below it."

So Vivienne did and she was amazed at how the colour easily blended with the first stroke.

"Put brown on your brush then dip it in a small bit of water the next stroke will be lighter. Continue doing this and you will see how the colour on your paper fades from dark brown at the top to very light brown at the bottom … useful when painting skies," he added.

Vivienne was lost in the excitement and joy of working with watercolour paints on watercolour paper.

She turned a glowing face towards Ivor. "This has rejuvenated me," she said.

"Oh yes," he said. "I can see that. Carry on, while I finish my painting."

Ivor had stopped to instruct Vivienne. "How would you like to do a small landscape all in that brown colour?"

Vivienne nodded, delighted.

"Then paint a very fine line right across the paper about two thirds of the way down, then starting at the top with a dark brown wash, continue making it lighter and lighter until you reach the line you painted. Then turn the paper upside down and make a similar wash, dark brown to very light at the point where the other wash stops. Then there is a hairdryer on the table. Use it to thoroughly dry your painting and I will tell you what to do next."

He nodded, as if expecting her to do as he had told her and got back to his own large painting of willow trees reflected in the still water of a lake. Vivienne soon was engrossed in doing as he had told her, wiping her sometimes too-wet brush on the piece of towelling and was starting to like what she was doing, though she felt a little anxious.

Ivor had looked at her.

"You need to enjoy it, Vivienne," he said, seeming to sense her nervousness. "Painting is enjoyable … it's therapy, too," he said, looking at her kindly.

Vivienne flushed slightly and realised that she had given no thought at all to Steven. She pulled herself back to the moment, the moment when she took the hairdryer in her hand, switched it on, and pointed the blower at her painting. Soon it was dry.

Ivor again stopped his painting.

"Now you paint big bold dark brown mountains above that line, and below it, a slim bendy path that is very narrow at the base of the mountains and broadens out as you get to the bottom of the paper. Perspective, you understand. The road from the mountains fades as it reaches the mountains. Then you can paint in a row of trees beside the road, also getting smaller and paler as they reach the mountains."

This occupied Vivienne for another half an hour but at the end of it, she was triumphant. She had a watercolour painting of a simple mountain scene all painted in shades of brown.

She smiled broadly at Ivor. And he smiled back.

"Happy, Vivienne?" he asked.

"Very happy," she said, "and what I really want to paint is the sunrise. It is so magical, navy night turning to bright sunshine in mere minutes. I could never compete with the universe in brilliance and colour, but I would love to spend time doing it.

"We will get there, Vivienne. It isn't that far off. Skies are large washes and you are just getting practice at doing large washes, then you need to practice with other colours. Now let's tidy up and you come and have a cup of coffee outside on the patio with me and tell me how you are so transformed. … you looked so heavy-laden last time I saw you and, today, you are different."

Vivienne felt different. She was doing her best to keep her mind uncluttered, to be aware, to be in the moment, and this painting session had been the best.

Sitting outside on the porch, she said, "On my way back to my house today I will stop at an art shop and buy brushes, paints and watercolour paper."

"Good, I'll give you a list of what to ask for," said Ivor. "But now tell me what was worrying you so badly the last time we sketched? And then we'll have some coffee and you can tell me what has happened to you to transform you …you are so different today!"

It was a direct question and Vivienne hesitated. This ws a very private matter for her, and she wasn't sure about this man. Could she trust him to listen without comment, to understand her pain, her distress at her son's transfer permanently to Paris whilst she remained in a strange town alone?

She decided to take the chance.

"Do you have children Ivor?" she ventured.

He looked surprised. "No, Vivienne. I have never married and I don't have children."

"If you did you might understand. I have an only son who I am very close to and it was his suggestion that brought me to Kalk Bay so I could be close to him, but now he has been transferred permanently to Paris. He left this morning and now I am alone here, after only three weeks, with no one I know and no direction in my life."

Ivor considered what she had said and nodded. "Yes, I can understand how that must have been a shock for you, Vivienne…. But the change in you? Your circumstances haven't changed, but you have."

"It was my visit to Lady Lavender that did it," she said.

"That witch," said Ivor in surprise.

"She is not a witch, Ivor. She is a very wise woman. She got me to see I was missing out on a happy life by immersing myself in depressing thoughts about my son."

"And how did she do that?" Ivor asked.

"She got me to understand that life is lived moment by moment, and that I needed to be aware of what I was thinking and of all that is around me and that, in that way, I would feel alive … and part of life as it were. Instead of this terrible sense of gloom I had sitting inside me. In fact, I don't even like talking about it."

Ivor laughed.

"You learnt the lesson well," he said.

"Why don't you come with me to visit her?" Vivienne asked.

"Me, visit her? I don't think so," said Ivor. "Not from what I've heard about her."

"Don't listen to rumours, Ivor," said Vivienne. She had a strong feeling Ivor would relate to Lady Lavender in some way, and hadn't she said he took the energy of her house to put in his paintings? She might like to find he was an artist and an ethical one at that.

"Somehow you think a bit like her, Ivor," said Vivienne. "You told me about needing a clear head when we were out sketching and that was why you go for walks, to clear your mind."

Ivor looked a little dubious.

"I just feel that I'd like you to meet her. She makes great biscuits," Vivienne added.

Ivor laughed. "I can't see myself visiting her at all, Vivienne. There would be no point in it."

"Okay, if you say so," said Vivienne, feeling disappointed, "but if I buy all the paints for a dawn painting, is there any way you could come to my house before dawn the day after tomorrow and help me with what I need to do to catch the dawn on watercolour paper?"

Ivor looked shocked. "You mean I would be walking in the dark to your house just to see the dawn break and to help you to paint it?"

"Why not?" said Vivienne. "It would be a new experience …. And I would love to know just how to go about doing that painting."

Vivienne didn't know how the idea had come to her or had the courage to suggest such a thing. A strange man to visit her just before dawn to show her how to paint a sky? Sounded ridiculous, but she was too old to be wanting Ivor for any other reason than to achieve a sudden desire to paint the magnificent skies that met her every morning.

"Besides I make the best coffee in town."

He laughed. "I guess I can do it," he conceded. "It's not dangerous walking in these streets at night. But you'll have to tell me where you live."

"It's easy to find. Opposite the railway station above the café, but I have a side entrance through the kitchen door, which is easier." She laughed. "This is exciting."

Ivor shook his head. "You have come a very long way, Vivienne, from the distressed woman you were only a few days ago."

Vivienne just knew that she could find a new path for her life in Kalk Bay… learning watercolour painting … if Ivor could guide her. She would not overburden him… well, just this once, she thought, and after that I will just get a book and learn from the book and work on my own.

"Deal," he said. They finished their coffee in silence. Ivor had got out a sheet of paper and was listing what she needed to buy to start her off on watercolour painting.

"And this is this book that will help you greatly," he said, writing down the title. "Most art shops will have it in stock."

Vivienne took the slip of paper, finished her coffee, thanked Ivor profusely for his help that morning.

"And don't forget your painting," said Ivor. "It will inspire you."

Vivienne walked briskly to the main street and the shops. She easily found an art supplier and enjoyed watching as the shopkeeper brought out small fat tubes of paint marked Ultramarine blue. Alizarin crimson, Cadmium yellow, Lemon yellow, Indian red, Cobalt blue, Prussian blue, Burnt amber and Paynes grey.

"No green?" she had said to Ivor.

"No, you mix it easily from blue and yellow, add some paynes grey and you'll get lovely shades of green."

Vivienne felt an excitement she hadn't felt in ages. Not even the thought of seeing Steven had given her this kind of excitement. The shopkeeper found the book Ivor had suggested, entitled *Big Brush Watercolour Painting*. When it came to buying the 300g watercolour paper, the A3 size frightened her. She wasn't ready for this big paper. She settled for two books of A4 paper and left for her home feeling even more joyous.

Back indoors, she went into the lounge and settled herself on the sofa … first she looked at all the tubes of paint, then she held the hake in her hands. It was new and slightly stiff, but she knew that wouldn't last for long. *Where was she going to paint?* The dining-room table, perhaps, but better still, would be to buy a small collapsible table she could put just in front of the window where she could see the night sky. She would do that tomorrow and be ready for Ivor's visit the following early morning. Satisfied with the day's outcome, she slept easily and peacefully, without a thought of Steven.

Chapter 8

Steven rang the next morning. "Just as you're having coffee, Mom," he said. "I worked out the time differences. How are you doing?"

There was too much to tell him, most of which he would not understand, so she said what most people say, "I'm fine, Steven."

There was a lift in her voice and Steven clearly noticed it for he said, "You sound good, Mom. I'm glad of that."

"How was your trip, darling…?"

When he rang off, she noticed she didn't dwell on Steven but got on with her day … her coffee, her shower and getting dressed. She was out after breakfast, looking for one of those little furniture shops she'd explored, hoping to find a small table she could use as her art table. There were a number of furniture shops on the main street and the first two couldn't help her. But the third one had just what she was looking for. A light-weight collapsible table about a metre in diameter when opened out. She paid for it and took it home, immediately opening it up under the window at which she liked to gaze at the dawn. Tomorrow morning, she would capture dawn on her paper. She found an old bit of towel, a jug for water and a cup to use for washing the brush between strokes.

She laid out the artists' palette, the twelve tubes of paint, the water jug and cup and brush along with the paper, all in readiness for five am tomorrow. And got on with the day.

Today it wasn't so bad. She had decided to bake some biscuits that she would enjoy nibbling in between meals and she would have something to offer Ivor the next day. Should she make chocolate chip cookies? Or her famous foam biscuits?

She decided on the foam biscuits which were light and easy to eat. She kept forgetting to watch herself and watch what she was doing, to be involved in the actions, but, mostly, she did remember. She found herself singing a song. Goodness, when had she last sung anything? And she was enjoying the cooking experience, mixing, tasting, rolling out, baking and smelling the delicious aroma of the biscuits as they baked.

She took them out and they were perfect. Slightly brown, soft to eat and tasty. Small enough to be a snack. She was having a happy day. The rest of it passed uneventfully, but when it came for time to sleep, Vivienne had trouble. Not for any other reason than excitement.

Painting the dawn, with an artist man! Whatever would Steven say? But Steven was in Paris and she was here. The thought didn't stay for long, but all the same, sleep was fitful and she was pleased to wake up well before dawn. She showered and got dressed, got out her cookies and was ready. She didn't doubt for a minute that Ivor would not come. He was trustworthy and reliable, she just knew it.

Although it was predawn, the street lights and shop lights threw a yellow light across everything, but if Vivienne looked at the sky over the railway station it was dark-navy. Perfect, she thought. That big brush I've just bought is going to get busy very soon!

Ivor was reliable and it was still before dawn when there was a knock on the kitchen door. Vivienne's heart missed several beats. What crazy thing have I done, she fleetingly wondered. But with a welcoming smile, she opened the outside door. A humourous face smiled at her.

"First time I've taken my walk to clear my head so early in the day," he quipped. "How are you, Vivienne?"

Vivienne stepped aside and ushered Ivor in to the small hallway. She closed and locked the door then turned around.

"Very well, thanks, Ivor. I've been so looking forward to this experience... and I'm all set up, come and see."

And she led him to the front of the house where she had set up her small table with her new paints, brushes, piece of towelling and cup of water. Ivor looked at it carefully.

"You learned it right, Vivienne. Everything you need is there, the cloth as well to wipe away excess water. Now where is our subject we are to paint?"

Vivienne felt a warmth about the way he said that. We are going to paint it, he'd said ... so he'd help her.

She also had put two chairs in position, one behind the art stuff and the other beside it. "There," she said, pointing at the window.

Beyond the window were the lights of the station but above and beyond that was a glimpse of the sheen of the moon on water, and above that, the endless expanse of a dark navy sky.

"Well, let's get started," said Ivor. "Nature doesn't wait, take some Prussian blue. That's a good dark colour to start with and put a bit of red with it, just to darken it further, and a touch of paynes grey. Now test it on the side of the paper. But first wash the top half with water so your paint flows easily."

He had bent forward to help her, His head of shaggy hair caught the light and she noticed that it had a faint golden sheen she hadn't seen before. This giant of a man was so sensitive and involved as he tested the colour.

"Good, Vivienne, now quickly brush the entire top half of your paper with this colour then below it, brush in some strokes of Indian red and cadmium yellow, because look, the first slivers of light are showing through the dark sky."

Vivienne noticed and it was all so exciting. She put her hake, first time to use it, into the big sloshy puddle of paint she had got on her palette and made long broad strokes across the white paper. Magically it was filling with a deep navy with a slight reddish touch, just what the rising sun was doing to the dark sky. Then below, after washing her brush, she brushed in some long strokes of yellow then some shorter ones of red, some more golden ones and some navy. How exciting it all was. She glanced at the sky which was rapidly getting lighter. Her painting didn't look much like it now but she had caught it before the sun peeped through.

Ivor was looking at the painting. "Good Vivienne, you've caught the predawn sky. Now for the sky line you can just paint in some dark shapes to represent the buildings ... I'll leave you to it."

It was all a very new experience and the big hake did put a lot of paint down very quickly. She used the dark Prussian blue with a bit of paynes grey to outline buildings against a predawn sky.

Ivor sat quietly watching her, smiling into his beard, she noticed.

Feeling suddenly bold, she put down her brush and smiled. "That was the best thing that has happened to me almost ever," she said. "Thank you, Ivor, for taking your walk so early!"

She was even able to be light in the way she spoke. What a great change for her! She looked with delight at the finished painting.

"I could have bought bigger paper," she said. "But it was intimidating. Maybe I'll go and buy A3 paper and try on my own to paint the dawn, but I couldn't have managed without you, Ivor," she said, adding, "Won't you have some coffee and a biscuit? I made them especially for you."

"Thank you. But let's put your painting up a bit further away so we can enjoy it," Ivor suggested. Picking up the block of paper with the painting still attached, he placed it on the windowsill and stood back to admire it.

"Yes, Vivienne, you can make it as an artist," he said. "You might even take your paintings to that coffee shop that keeps mine."

A feeling of huge joy flooded Vivienne. Could she really have found something she would really enjoy doing? Maybe she wasn't quite ready to take in paintings to the coffee shop but given her enthusiasm and love of skies, she could have endless fun with clouds … and heavy dark days, too.

She smiled at Ivor.

"My son told me it would be so much better here. I was sincerely doubting that. But this morning has revived my belief that this really could be true. I would never be doing this at home." The sun had risen and it was time for coffee.

"Coffee now, Ivor?" she asked. "I really do make a good cup."

"Love some, thanks, Vivienne," he said, following her into the kitchen.

Vivienne had such strong feelings of joy she hadn't had in ages. Or ever. She was living in the moment,…before she had not been living at all, really, filled with worry and thoughts of having made a mistake and more thoughts of losing Steven. Right now, she had a new friend, an artist, following her into her small bright kitchen. She turned and smiled at him. "There's a chair if you'd like to wait. I even have cream if you'd like it in your coffee."

She looked directly at him as he sat in the chair. He looked back at her and his crinkly smile behind the beard showed itself momentarily.

"Such delicacies," he said.

"It's not always like this," said Vivienne as she turned on the coffee maker. "But I got cream in specially for Steven the day before yesterday."

"Your son?"

"Yes, that one, left for Paris to live there." She said this with a tone of regret.

Ivor looked at her.

"He'll have a marvellous time," he said. "I've lived and painted in Paris."

"You have?"

"Yes, being a bachelor, it has been easy for me to travel the world and to paint in various places. But I like it here."

Vivienne had a chance to find out more about Ivor. The coffee was boiling, but she halted pouring it into two mugs to ask, "What brought you to Kalk Bay?"

"Nothing deliberate. Life is full of happy accidents. I had another car at that time and it broke down in this village. So that is how I got to know the tow-truck owner, the garage owner, a nice bed and breakfast and the coffee shop that keeps my paintings now."

Vivienne poured the two mugs of coffee. He paused to put cream and sugar into his coffee that Vivienne handed him. Then he took a sip and smiled at Vivienne. "This coffee is good," he said and then continued, "That man told me about a house to rent, the one I'm in now. That was four years ago and I am completely happy here. The sea, the mountains, the artists in the village, everything. It suits me perfectly."

"And you need to go for daily walks," said Vivienne. "I thank you for taking your walk to me this morning."

"Yes, my walks, including walks at predawn." He smiled at her. "But I've enjoyed this morning, Vivienne, and we need to paint together sometimes out of doors. I can help you to develop."

These were the best words Vivienne had heard in a long time. Suddenly, the move to Kalk Bay didn't seem so stupid, after all. She wanted to hug Ivor but thought that he might take offense, so she just smiled and thanked him for his kindness. Both he and Vivienne were silent as they drank their coffee, but there was a warm feeling in her kitchen. And when Ivor put down his empty cup and stood up to leave, she put her hands on his shoulders and thanked him again … "I didn't think life was worth living a couple of days ago," she said. "But this paint and painting … with your help … has given me wings to fly!"

"Steady on," said Ivor, smiling, as he turned to leave. "Flying is great, but keeping one's feet on the ground is very helpful."

He gave her a little wave and was gone. Vivienne sat with her heart full of joy, and before she washed the cups, she made a trip to the lounge to look at the night sky painting. It had dried and was a bit paler, but it still had a wonderful quality of the sky before dawn. *What joy!*

Chapter 9

Vivienne didn't have any doubts as to what she was going to do that day. She was going to take her painting to Lady Lavender, to thank her for helping her to make sense of her life by living it, one moment at a time. She shook her head. What a different person she had become! Would Lady Lavender mind a visit? She knew that she would not.

She knew the way there and was observant as she walked. Watched a seagull in flight and listened to its plaintive cries, smiled at a large baboon eating fruit off a tree, watched a tiny mouse skuttle into the undergrowth. There was so much that she was seeing today she had not seen before that it made her smile. We are all connected, she thought. Somehow.

The path seemed shorter and the glimpse of the brilliant blue of the sea with its white frills of breaking waves lifted her spirits even higher. What could compare with views like this? She breathed in deeply the slightly salty sea air. There was a faint breeze just ruffling the leaves, cooling the air. All in all, Vivienne was delighted with life. She held under one arm, the rolled-up painting of the early dawn sky. Her first.

Around the corner she saw the slightly crooked walls of the fisherman's cottage, the glorious roses on the trellis and the large bushes of lavender. Of course, Lady Lavender. She smiled as she knocked on the door.

The door opened almost instantly and Lady Lavender in a long dress of lavender was there to greet her. The gimlet eyes took in everything, Vivienne knew. Lady Lavender looked affable as she smiled slightly at Vivienne.

"I've been expecting you, Vivienne."

"Again!" said Vivienne in surprise.

"Yes, but do come in. Let's get some ginger tea and I'm ready to listen. I can see you have a lot to tell me."

How wonderful it was to have an ear that would listen, thought Vivienne, even if I do get a lecture… but the lectures have done me good, she thought.

Vivienne smiled to herself. She was getting used to this greeting.

"This time it's ginger biscuits made with real ginger to have with our ginger tea.."

Soon she and Lady Lavender were seated comfortably in the lounge with tea and biscuits. Vivienne saw Lady Lavender looking at her expectantly.

"So Vivienne, what have you to report?" she asked after each had had a sip of tea.

Vivienne was relaxed as she said, "I've never felt this excited about life before, Lady Lavender. Suddenly every moment has become precious and I'm seeing things around me I've never seen before. It was like I've been sleep walking until now." she paused for breath.

Lady Lavender sat, silently, waiting as Vivienne continued, "It's been difficult to keep watching what I think and to bring it back to the moment and watching where I am and what I am doing, but this morning I painted the sunrise. Not as beautifully as nature does it, but it is so exciting for me. Let me show you." She unfurled the rolled-up piece of paper and flattened it, taking it over to where lady lavender was sitting.

"Sit beside me, Vivienne," she invited, "then you can show me better."

So Lady Lavender moved over on the sofa and Vivienne sat next to her. She gave off the faintest perfume of lavender and Vivienne again smiled to herself. *What an unusual woman!*

"So, let me see," said Lady Lavender.

The paint had dried even more and in the top section of the dark navy sky there were patches of light, as if the sun was trying to break through. And in the bottom half, were daring streaks of red and gold, and yellow as that bright orb broke through the navy of night. It was clearly an early-morning dawn sky and Lady Lavender nodded.

"You have caught its energy, Vivienne, a lovely light energy for a glorious day ahead for you," she said. "And this is good in a painting. If you carry on, you will give this energy to those people who view your paintings. Or," she added, with a smile, "buy them."

"That's what is so exciting, Lady Lavender," said Vivienne. "I don't need to make a living. I have enough to live on, but I have found a purpose for my life. Something I didn't have and that is to learn what I can about watercolour painting and to paint."

"That's good news," said Lady Lavender.

"It is," said Vivienne, "and I've also made friends with Ivor, the artist who painted a picture of your house. He came to help me paint the dawn and I do want to bring him here to meet you. You seem to say the same things. He talks of an empty mind and letting the paint decide where to go, as if it had a life of its own."

Lady Lavender nodded. "He's right, you know," she said. "It does have. Everything is energy, paint as well, and if you connect with the field the painting does itself. I do understand that."

"Then can I bring him here to meet you?" asked Vivienne. "Both you and he have made such a difference to my life. It is exciting and I feel alive now."

"Are you not worried about your son?"

Vivienne was momentarily startled. "You know, Lady Lavender, I haven't thought about him at all. Is that a bad thing?"

"Of course not," said Lady Lavender. "By constantly thinking of him, you would be getting in the way of his natural development.

Let him go, Vivienne, let him be free to follow his stars, as you are doing."

"Oh yes," said Vivienne. "And what is truly amazing is that I understand now what Steven told me it is true: it is so much better here. I don't think he meant physically, either. I think he meant spiritually. I didn't see the meaning until just now."

Lady Lavender just smiled.

"You have heard the saying, when the student is ready, the teacher will appear. We have had connections before, Vivienne, but I am not going into that. Yes, you are most welcome to bring Ivor here. It would be good to find out what kind of energy he has put into the painting of my house."

She continued. "My work is rewarding to me, too, Vivienne. I work on a different level, helping humanity to clear up the disasters it makes and to lift people's heaviness by helping them to let go of the past and to live just in the moment. We lift our energies and that of the whole planet to bring in a whole new lightness and happiness for us all, animals and plants included." She nodded and Vivienne, sitting next to her, felt a shaft of huge energy pass through her. Lifting her, she thought, to stay in this new wonderous world where there was so much good and so much to be grateful for.

Chapter 10

Back in her house, Vivienne did a bit of quick house-cleaning then sat in her lunge absorbed in the book on big-brush watercolour painting. It was so explicit, she understood exactly what to do, but she needed bigger paper. A4 was too small. A3 and later, even A2, but she would start with A3 paper and a lot more paints and spend time indoors painting, she thought. Thoughts of taking Ivor to see Lady Lavender had faded in her excitement at paging through this book. The wet into wet looked marvellous. Misty outlines of trees in the background with stronger misty trees in the foreground and some very strong details right up front. She knew now how to mix the paints, and tried with the yellows, blues and paynes grey to produce a work of different shades of green, going from the bright light green of a new spring leafy tree to the dark green of old leaves … it was thrilling. And time just flew.

Vivienne soon had a number of pages of A4 paper filled up with broad strokes, mostly of pale blue with the misty green of background trees, but later, she experimented with the sea. Again the big brush was amazing and very quickly produced the impression of a distant ocean with small white breakers in it … using that scrambling technique she had accidently first used … to create sparkles on the water. Vivienne didn't know life could be such fun!

Steven phoned from Paris. She was glad to hear his voice, but she didn't try to keep him on the phone and didn't dwell on his call as he hung up. He was settling and happy. She was settling and happy.

After a day in which most of the sheets of the A3 pad had paint on them she remembered Ivor and had the feeling, once again, that she would like him and Lady Lavender to meet. She didn't know why. Tomorrow, that would be her mission. Today was rich and full with her own efforts and what she was glad about was that she was taking control of her own life.

The next morning when Steven phoned from Paris in a light voice she was glad to tell him… "Steven, you were so right when you told me that it was so much better here. I am finding that to be true."

Steven sounded surprised. "Really, Mom?" he asked. "I'm delighted to hear that. I have been so worried about you alone in Kalk Bay."

"No worry, Steven, this is the best thing that could have happened to me."

Steven had a light tone to his voice as he said, "Whew, Mom, I'm so glad, because you can't know how much I am enjoying Paris. Everything. The culture, the way of life, my work and, of course, Mariette." He said it with such warmth that this time Vivienne noticed that she really was pleased for him.

"I'm happy for you, Steven. That you are having this adventure and have found your ideal girl."

"Oh yes, Mom, everything about her. She even cooks divinely!"

Vivienne chuckled to herself. The way to a man's heart is through his stomach, she remembered, but, of course, he had found Mariette before he found she could cook.

So the day had started well. Vivienne had greeted the dawn, talked to Steven and had breakfast and was off … in search of Ivor.

She found him about to start a new painting.

"Please can you delay it, Ivor?" she asked. "Please come with me to meet Lady Lavender. I just know you have something in common. You speak about an empty mind and so does she."

Ivor was not easy to persuade.

"But, Vivienne, I have my morning laid out," he said. "And I really don't think this is necessary."

"For me, it is," urged Vivienne. "Both you and Lady Lavender have encouraged such changes in my life."

"You want me to try out her biscuits to compare them to yours?" said Ivor, seeming to relax a little and even seeing some humour in the situation.

"It's not funny, Ivor," said Vivienne. "You have made great changes for me. I've painted pages of paper with the hake and pools of paint. I'm happier than I've ever been, but Lady Lavender also helped me with changes. I don't know why I want you to meet her. Perhaps so you don't think she's a witch."

"Those are my private thoughts, Vivienne," said Ivor.

Vivienne looked at the large man in his smock that covered his clothes. She noticed that he was beginning to take it off and she smiled to herself. He's coming, she thought. She didn't know what would transpire. She didn't know why she wanted them to meet, except that for her it was now her stable footing in a new village she now called Home.

Ivor exchanged his artist's smock for his loose overcoat. And he looked at Vivienne.

"Let's go," he said, indicating she go out of the door whilst he locked up.

It was a long walk to the fisherman's cottage, but as it was mostly downhill Vivienne kept up with Ivor's long strides. They didn't talk as they walked. Vivienne pulled her mind back to the moment, watching as she walked and looking at what was around her, noticing details and colours she had never noticed before, and appreciating it all. Soon came the glint of the sun on the water and, a bit later, they went down the last few steps and there it was – the fisherman's cottage. Vivienne glanced at Ivor. Even under the beard she could see a rigid set to his face. What was going to be the outcome of this? she wondered.

Ivor pointed to the knocker. "You knock," he said.

126

Vivienne's heart was beating fast; she did so. In a short while, there was the eye looking through the spy hole. It stared at them for half a minute then the door slowly opened. Inside the doorway, in the usual long dress, but this one pure white, stood Lady Lavender, to meet them.

Lady Lavender gave her usual greeting, "Good morning, Vivienne, I've been expecting you." She looked pointedly at Ivor.

Vivienne hurried to say, "Lady Lavender, this is Ivor, the artist who painted your cottage. I'm sorry if we are intruding, but I wanted you to meet him. May we please come in?"

Lady Lavender barely hesitated before standing to one side and ushering them inside. "I think the kitchen is the first place, Vivienne," she said. "We can get our ginger tea and this time its cinnamon cookies. How do you like cinnamon?" This she addressed to Ivor. Vivienne had the feeling Lady Lavender expected her to like anything she was presented with.

Ivor looked a bit surprised. "Cinnamon and I get on very well," he said in his fairly deep voice. Then he added politely, "Thank you."

Lady Lavender looked at him. "Any friend of Vivienne's is welcome here. In this kitchen, we brew our special tea. Ginger tea with honey. Would you like that?"

"Yes, thank you," said Ivor, still very formal. Vivienne watched Lady lavender cut slices off a large root of ginger and place them in three delicate china cups. She added boiling water and after it had momentarily cooled, added a large spoon of honey to each.

"Now we are equipped," she said, "Please take some biscuits then let us go and sit in my lounge where it is comfortable."

Leading the way, she ushered them into her sparsely furnished lounge. As usual, she sat on the sofa, and indicated to Vivienne and Ivor to each take a chair.

She looked at Ivor. Vivienne saw her penetrating dark eyes,

which seemed to spark slightly, observing him. The large black cat had appeared and she stroked it and spoke directly to it. "Captain, this is Ivor, a friend of Vivienne's and means no harm."

The cat seemed to understand and squatted next to her, tail curled around its paws, looking directly at Ivor.

"Are you sure *that cat* means no harm?" he asked, looking at Captain, who was still looking at him.

"Oh yes," said Lady Lavender. "He checked you out when you were sitting on that log painting and the report came back that you meant no harm. But I am glad to meet you, because the energy of this cottage would be in your painting and I wanted to see you had the right energy to deal with the very fine energy that lives in this old house."

Both Vivienne and Ivor looked at her, but said nothing.

Lady Lavender nodded as she observed Ivor.

"Yes, a good man," she said. "Good enough to be blessed with the pure energies of this old cottage. So much has happened here … perilous lives lost on the ocean, babies' births in this cottage, hardships, love and joy, all have inhabited this house, but fine energies developed as the descendants learned to love life and the sea and to cherish each other and to care for the ocean, taking only what they needed for their daily survival.

"Each generation grew stronger and connected more with the collective, benefiting not only themselves, but others around them. They learnt to read and to write and to teach others the same valuable skills. They learnt to cook and passed these skills on as well. I learnt from my mother and she from her mother and we have become strong and depend now not on outside sources such as television and radio, but on what is given to us by spirit. By our intuition." She stopped there. "I would like Ivor to tell us about himself."

This is what Vivienne had been waiting for. What would now

128

transpire?

Ivor said, "I didn't want to visit as quite honestly there is talk that you are a witch."

Vivienne was appalled, but Lady Lavender smiled. "They may be right," she said. "But not all witches are evil."

Ivor looked nonplussed. It was obvious he hadn't expected her to agree with him,

"Yes, I do have influence over the weather," said Lady Lavender, "though I prefer to let the elements work out what they want. But if things are getting badly out of hand, I am able to calm things down. So, no I am not a witch but a psychic working for the good of mankind."

Vivienne spoke quickly. "What made me feel I wanted Ivor to talk with you was the way both he and you told me about awareness and having a quiet mind, though each said it in different ways. Ivor needs to clear his head before he paints, and you tell me I am to watch my thoughts and to stay in the moment. Also, to get a peaceful head. And both your truths have helped me," she said. "So I just wanted you to meet. I am new here and have had such help from both of you."

"Ivor has been teaching you to paint I take it," said Lady lavender. She nodded to Ivor. "Yesterday, she brought to me her painting of the dawn of a new day."

"Which is that I feel is happening to me," Vivienne said. "I do feel a newness I have never experienced before."

"Rather not talk about it," said Lady Lavender. "You scatter your energies. Rather just *know* it is happening."

She looked at Ivor. "Would you like to tell us how you developed your relationship with spirit?"

Ivor looked startled then seemed to relax. "From the time I was fourteen years old, I wanted to paint. I couldn't find teachers who could help. If I wanted to paint a red sky, I felt I should be allowed to, but one school of art told me skies are blue. So I left that teacher. Eventually, I found a man who taught me so much about light and colour, about the density of rays, and how to make light appear in a painting by the way I mixed paints and the way one colour stood next to another. This man was a magician with paint. And I learnt what I could from him, then went my own way. That often meant being almost penniless and hungry. One learns a lot about trusting intuition and the universe when one is down to nothing and yet help arrives in unexpected ways.

So, early on, I learnt about the value of silence, of being quiet and of being aware. Of having an empty mind. And being ready, when the spark ignited in me the need o paint …. I began to sell my paintings and later could afford to stay where I liked and wasn't ever hungry for food again. Though always hungry for new experiences, or new ideas of what to paint." He stopped at this point, looked around and then continued, "So I have approached my quiet mind though my art, my work."

Lady Lavender was almost smiling. "Vivienne, you have a great teacher in Ivor. He is going to help you to become a good artist yourself, I know."

Vivienne was delighted. This visit was turning out to be a success.

"And I will be here to oversee you both," concluded Lady Lavender. "I don't even need to see you in the physical. I can follow your energies and find you wherever you are and help to direct your paths. They could in some way merge." And she smiled.

Merge? What did she mean? wondered Vivienne.

"Didn't you say your son said it would be so much tetter here?" Lady Lavender said. "You have already told me you felt he was right."

"Yes, but not in the physical sense," said Vivienne. "I feel that in my inner being it is so much better here. Inside me, I mean."

"Yes," said Lady Lavender, "but I'm sure you've heard it said that the inner becomes the outer, just as the outer becomes the inner."

She looked at Lady Lavender with a puzzled expression and saw the smile that crossed her face. She knows something I don't thought Vivienne…

The next day, Vivienne was as usual up early to watch the sunrise, which was getting a little later as winter slowly approached. She had showered and dressed and had the coffee boiling with the strong aroma wafting out into the small lane outside her kitchen window when she heard footsteps. Not the quick ones of Steven, but rather slower more leisurely footsteps approaching and then there was a knock on her kitchen door.

Vivienne was momentarily shocked. Who was knocking? And so early in the morning? She didn't have a spy hole as Lady Lavender had, so she cautiously unlocked the door to look into the amused face of Ivor.

"Ivor," she said, "you startled me. Taking a walk so early in the morning?"

"Yes," he said, "from my house I could smell the aroma of that lovely coffee that you make, so I wondered if you might let me join you for that early-morning cuppa."

Vivienne was overjoyed and quickly opened the door. She hugged Ivor.

"Hey steady on," he said. "What's the excitement?"

Vivienne stepped back and stopped smiling. Then she said seriously, "You might not understand, but I have so enjoyed this early morning cup of coffee in the presence of my son. It has been lonely now that he's in Paris, but I'm getting used to it. The coffee is still good."

"Yes, I know and that why I am here."

Vivienne smiled again. "Sorry I was over excited, Ivor, but it was so nice having you to coffee a few mornings ago. Such a pleasure and when I heard a knock and didn't know who it was, and then saw it was you, I did get excited. Please come in," With a flourish she stood aside for the big man to enter

Vivienne noticed his hair was very neatly brushed this morning and the early morning light caught the golden glint again. His hazel eyes were flickering with amusement, as he followed her into the kitchen and seated himself.

"I haven't only come for coffee, Vivienne," he said. "I do have a car which I seldom use, but I drove here this morning. And I thought you might like to come on an early-morning painting trip with me, perhaps to the other side of this peninsula to the beaches of Kommetjie ... on the west coast where the waves are bigger. Not that we will be swimming. Would that suit you, Vivienne? We might eat a few biscuits with our coffee and, later, get a late breakfast somewhere on that side of the peninsula."

Vivienne spirits were fairly lifting her out of the kitchen and she felt enormous joy. To be doing something she had just found she loved doing with this nice sensitive artist who could help her and he was offering to drive her to the other side of the peninsula to paint an early-morning sea scene.

"I guess the sunrise happens on this side, but there will still be the sparkle of the sun on the water and the light in the early morning is excellent for painting," he said. "'How does this strike you as an idea?"

"Oh the best ever idea," said Vivienne, opening the packet of milk rusks and the tin of her special foam biscuits. "Let me gather my painting equipment into a bag, Ivor and I'll be with you in minutes."

She quickly found a hat and a wind-cheater and her bag of paints and paper and water jar and cloth.

"All right," she said. "I'm ready."

Ivor was finishing his coffee and eating her foam biscuits. "Very good, Vivienne," he said.

"Yes, let me eat a couple of biscuits myself just to keep away the hunger pangs," she said.

Not much later, she locked the back door and, with Ivor carrying her bag of paints, followed him down the steps to a handsome dark-blue Mercedes sports car that stood in the narrow lane.

"I like the feel of the wind in my hair," he chuckled, "but if you want me to pull over the roof top, let me do so."

"Oh no," said Vivienne. "This is the first time I will be travelling in an open car. Let me see how I feel about the wind in my hair." She laughed, knowing it was short and would not be a problem in the wind.

Soon they were on their way, finding the route that would take them over the mountains to the coast line on the other side. Vivienne smiled to herself as the wind tousled her short, bobbed hair and whisked Ivor's shoulder-length hair backwards.

She laughed. "This is such fun, Ivor," she shouted above the wind. "Thank you so much."

"Oh yes a convertible is the best," he said. "It wouldn't be good for business, but, for me, as an artist enjoying the occasional trip into the interior or further down the coast just with my paints and time to please myself, it is perfect."

Vivienne thought so as well. And though she was still in the moment and very aware she was also aware that this was proving to be exactly what Steven said it would be. Didn't he tell her, it's so much better here? And wasn't it, both within and now without, as well? Vivienne looked at the big man driving and he turned and caught her eye and they smiled at one another. A bond had been sealed in that moment. No longer was it an artist and his student. It was two good friends who understood one another and supported each other where they could.

The powerful sports car had reached the top of the row of hills and now there was a view down the other side … to the West Coast. They had driven up the mountains on this side when they drove to reach Cape Point, but now the journey was simply straight across to reach the beach and the sea.

Vivienne caught her breath. The sunlight glinting on the sea sparkled and, in the distance, she could see long breakers endlessly splashing onto white sand. Or it looked white from where they were. The car wound down a long hill, past houses and shops and then found its way down a narrow road that ended in a sandy carpark.

"We'll park here," said Ivor, "but I'll roll up the roof and lock the car. It will be safer. But let's get out our art things first." Soon the car was locked and Ivor was carrying both their bags of artists materials.

"Look there's a café there," said Ivor, "so we can have a quick breakfast before we start. Would you like that, Vivienne?" He put special emphasis on her name and it felt good.

"Beautiful," said Vivienne, looking at the view. "And I would most certainly enjoy a good breakfast." She smiled at Ivor. "Those few biscuits are long forgotten."

He smiled back at her, his hazel eyes glinting with amusement. "Food is important to you, isn't it, Vivienne?"

They had pushed open the small gate and were walking along the path leading to the cafe. As they walked ,Vivienne replied, "It's not that I eat all the time, Ivor, but unlike you, when your paints are the most important things in your life, I like food. The different sorts of dishes, the ingredients, the recipes, the making and the cooking and ..." she laughed, "...and of course the eating, too. If you visit me at dinnertime, I'll cook you something delicious …

even if you are a light eater, you'll enjoy my dishes. I love the kitchen."

They entered the cafe, and found a table in the corner. The smells of food cooking reminded them both why they were there.

A waiter was almost at their table with the menu as Ivor leant over towards Vivienne and said, "That's a date and I'll maybe begin to care more about food and even about myself." He chuckled. "But you have to prove it to me, Vivienne. When should I come to sample delicious food that takes me out of my rut … yes, I know I'm in a rut."

Vivienne thought to herself, what an admission … she was running through her head some tasty dishes he would like … so she was slightly hesitant before she replied, "Say the day after tomorrow in the evening? I'll do my best to take you out of your rut."

They smiled fondly at one another.

"Meantime, have you studied the breakfast menu," said Ivor, taking the menu from the waiter. "Listen to the variety… hash browns, omelettes with herbs and mushrooms, or bacon … or eggs or toasted sandwiches … what would be a good start to a day of good painting? I'm going for the sausage, chips, eggs. bacon and mushrooms."

"No," said Vivienne, "I'm for a cheese omelette today with some extra fillings … maybe ham." She looked at the waiter who was writing down their order.

"And coffee? Would you like that now?" asked the waiter.

"Why not," said Ivor. "For me it's a cup of strong coffee."

"And for me a Cappuccino," said Vivienne.

The waiter nodded and moved off.

"See how different we are," said Ivor.

"Not different, Ivor, just individuals. I think that's good. It would be boring if we both liked the same things. Nothing to argue about." Vivienne said that with a smile.

"Not argue," said Ivor. "I would not like to start arguing with you, Vivienne."

"Alright discussing is perhaps a better word."

"Or comparing," said Ivor.

"There you go, choice of language," said Vivienne.

They continued with easy banter until the coffee arrived and shortly after that, their breakfasts. Neither spoke as they ate, but both smiled as they finished.

"Now to find the right spot to paint those masterpieces," said Ivor. "It's probably best if we just sit on one of those sand dunes and have easy access to our painting materials."

Ivor had settled the bill and they had strolled out along the path and through the gate; they were now on the beach, which was strewn with seaweed, shells and bits of driftwood. The sand dunes were the best places to sit on, as, though there were rocks, they were far away. And there were some trees at the edge of the sand dunes.

Both settled comfortably on a sand dune beneath the shade of a tree and each spread out the materials they'd be using. Luckily, Vivienne's paper was on a block, which meant it was stable, thick and the pages wouldn't blow away in the slight breeze. She had her water in a screw top jar and had sensibly only brought along three brushes. The hake which Ivor had taught her to use and to love, a rigger with a very fine point and a round brush, which could prove useful.

There was an interesting rocky outcrop a bit further along the beach and the waves were hitting against it, spraying sparkling foam into the air. Could she capture that on paper? she wondered. It was what caught her eye.

Ivor, she, saw was looking at the sky, which had lovely curling white clouds in it. She didn't spend much time watching Ivor, as, very soon, she was immersed in her own painting. No, the sky was not her main interest, so her sky line was high … her main interest was the great spraying foam against the shining black rocks, with a bit of pale white sand and the brilliance of a very blue sea. It was a challenge, but Vivienne remembered to paint well one mustn't think, one must soak up the scene, immerse oneself in it, become it, become the rocks and the wave hitting the rocks and then with the colours, she'd put out on her palette, let her brush work its magic.

She was soon completely part of what she was painting, unaware of how the paint was going on the paper and that there was an amazing big splash of shimmering white spray that she had caught. Ivor, too, was immersed in what he was doing … Almost in unison both looked up when they had finished and smiled that smile that wasn't just a smile … it was a bond of affection and love of what they were doing .,, and maybe even love for each other … .

Two days later, Vivienne had bought aromatic eucalyptus oil and winter green, mixed then and set them in a small container with a candle beneath to give off s subtly aromatic smell. She had set the dining-room table with two place settings with a single daisy in a small vase. Altogether the setting looked elegant and she was pleased.

She was also pleased with the chicken a la king dish she had made. She had an excellent recipe that needed cream, mushrooms, green pepper, and chicken breasts cooked lightly in butter. The completed dish was further enhanced with just the right amount of sherry.

Vivienne had made a salad, had bought fresh rosemary bread and had made an apple pie to be served with thick cream. She had placed wine glasses at each table setting and had three different bottles of red wine. She stood back with pride to view her handiwork.

As good as the best, she thought, glad to be entertaining Ivor for dinner and taking him out of his so-called rut. On time, she heard the car arrive, the door shut, the ping of the alarm and then the regular and steady footsteps of Ivor. She was at the door with a smile to meet him, and ushered him first into the lounge. She had set out an entrée of small pieces of toast with pate and some cheesy biscuits to nibble.

Ivor looked at it all. "This takes me out of my rut," he said. "Very different from what I serve myself with."

"Ah, that's not the best. That is still to come," she said in a conspiratorial whisper.

Ivor laughed.

"Vivienne did you also take acting classes?" he asked. "Because the audience would love that line."

Vivienne laughed. "Do sit down, Ivor, and tell me how your day was."

"Well, I spent a bit of time admiring my painting of the sea from the other day, so tranquil, yet with so much mystery and depth, and the clouds I caught are spectacular. Yes, it was a good day with good painting." He stopped and looked at Vivienne.

"And how you caught the sparkles on that huge wave amazed me."

"Oh, it was my first experience with the big brush that taught me how to make shiny spots on paper… dry scramble, I think you called it."

Ivor laughed and patted Vivienne on the shoulder. "You are a great academic, Vivienne, besides being a great actress. But you did an amazing job catching the light on that wave."

"I've been too busy to look at my painting," said Vivienne. "I even picked a daisy growing just outside my door, which you will see on the dining-room table when we go in for a meal, which I hope you will enjoy."

They sat for a while longer, nibbling biscuits and enjoying small glasses of sherry Vivienne had also provided. Then they went through to the dining room, where Vivienne had dimmed the lights.

The first thing Ivor did was to wrinkle up his nose. "Aromatic oils," he said.

"Yes, that's right," said Vivienne. "I hope you aren't allergic or anything …."

"No, not at all. It's all very pleasant, thanks, Vivienne. And, in the half-light, Ivor smiled as he spied the dining-room table correctly set with cutlery plates and glasses.

"The best of the best," he said. "Thank you, Vivienne."

Vivienne smiled in the dimmed light. "I had fun, Ivor. They say that cooking needs an audience. To go to a lot of trouble just for oneself is not exciting, but I had a wonderful time preparing this for you. Please sit down whilst I bring along the dishes."

Ivor sat, taking his table napkin and spreading it on his lap. He shook his head. "Vivienne, you do amaze me," he said.

"More so when you enjoy this food," said Vivienne, carrying in the serving dish of chicken a la king and of rice. The salads and bread were already on the table.

"And Ivor the white wine is in the fridge. Do you mind fetching it, please? And here on the table is the red wine, which I know doesn't get chilled."

Ivor obliged and soon they were clinking glasses and smiling as they toasted each other.

"Now to try out my special dish," said Vivienne. "Please help yourself… and there's bread on the table as well." Very soon both were enjoying what was a first-rate dish. Ivor was impressed and said so.

"Definitely, I'm out of my rut," he said. "What have I been missing with food like this?"

"Oh, and there's apple tart and cream still to come," said Vivienne.

Whilst they ate, they chatted. Ivor told Vivienne about some of the cities he had lived in and painted in, and how his life had unfolded, eventually bringing him back to South Africa.

"It's my home, one's roots as it were, and I'm quite content in Kalk Bay," he said. "True it is an artist's paradise... musicians, artists, writers, jewellers, they are all here. And the sea makes it perfect. I don't think I've been missing anything ..." he hesitated "...Well, maybe I have."

He looked at Vivienne as he said this.

Vivienne felt a great surge of joy. She had never thought of having a man in her life again, not at her age. Of course, Steven had said she was still young and could start again, but she remembered she got angry with him... Never expecting that one day she might want to make another start ... to perhaps have a life with Ivor.

She didn't know how he felt. Perhaps not the same as she did, but she could see he was appreciating her efforts that night, and appreciating her as well. She felt the effort had been well worth it. They both relaxed, enjoyed the dessert, and the coffee that followed.

"And do you want me to stay and help you clean up?" asked Ivor.

Vivienne was pleasantly surprised. "No, Ivor, not at all, that's part of the ceremony, though," she added with a smile. "That's one thing I have to get used to; here I look after everything ... back in Cowies Hill, I had domestic help."

"You could here, too," said Ivor.

"No," said Vivienne, "I have nothing much to do all day so a bit of housework is excellent to help fill in my time, though now I've got painting. …" and she nearly added, "…and you."

She didn't, though to herself she did, because she knew that he felt for her what she was feeling for him.

As he left it was maybe a surprise to both of them when he put his arms around her and leant down and gently kissed her. A long kiss that held a lot of meaning.

"Thank you, Vivienne, for a wonderful night. "And," he added with a small smile, "thank you for our first kiss."

His eyes met hers and held them as her heart thumped inside her chest. His eyes seemed to be speaking to her as she gazed back at him. Then he smiled at her, nodded and walked to the back door and out of it.

Vivienne stood, with a bemused look on her face as she heard his car start up. What was happening to her? She was experiencing feelings for Ivor that were strong and even passionate. Had she fallen in love with him? And he with her? It seemed that way…

Printed in the United States
by Baker & Taylor Publisher Services